Forever

By

Design

~A NOVEL~

ELIZABETH
JAMES

DESIGN SERIES #3

Edited by Kathy Krick

Cover photo ©2013 Elizabeth James/Personal Photos

Cover design by Maria DeSouza

DEDICATION

To Sissy and Bobby- I feel like you've been with me throughout this journey and when I've been nervous or doubted I could finish, I carried on with your inspiration and determination as my guide. I miss you both every day.

~with all my love

THANK YOUS:

There are so many people I want to thank but first and foremost, my husband. I love you and I appreciate your letting me follow my dream.

I also want to thank my mom and dad for being the best support a person could have and the rest of my family for being there for me.

I want to thank my "sisters" who I carry in my heart every day. I love y'all and am blessed to have you in my life.

I am also blessed to have a wonderful friend in Kassie Baker who has now endured three books with me and she hasn't killed me yet. Thank you for knowing me better than I know myself sometimes and keeping me sane. I love ya!

I'm so happy to have worked with Kathy Krick on this book as my friend and my editor. Kathy, you're great at what you do and I thank you from the bottom of my heart.

Thank you to Maria DeSouza for your help in bringing my cover to life. It's amazing how a photo I shot walking through downtown Raleigh, NC could become such a gorgeous cover. You amaze me.

To my beta readers, Jodi Negri and Kassie Baker…thank you for keeping my words in the right places and also for giving your awesome feedback. You both seem to know my thoughts better than I do.

To my amazing author friends who share my love of writing, I thank you. I'm so proud of all of you and am a big fan! Thank you for all of your cross-promotion and support!

To my E. James Street Team: You girls are my sounding board, my support, my entertainment, and my biggest cheerleaders. I love each and every one of you and am so blessed to have you as a part of my team.

Prologue

Tyler

I want to give her the papers myself. I'm hoping that when she sees me face to face she'll realize she still loves me. I've brought along my buddy, Mark to back me up in case there's any trouble with pretty boy but as the car drives up I see she isn't driving, her new man is. I can feel my stomach turn as I watch him get out of her car knowing that he's the one with my family instead of me. I've parked my car away from them but I can hear their conversation through the partially open window. Jolene, climbing from the back of the car runs to grab his hand calling him daddy. Daddy? She's calling HIM daddy? I look over at Mark who gives me a sympathetic smile as I give him the envelope. He tucks it in his jacket and I tell him to make sure Jane's alone before giving it to her. I watch him sprint across the parking lot coming up right behind her. He startles her. I see him speaking and she seems afraid. Mark is blatantly checking her out and it ticks me off. I hear him tell her that I sent a message and he hands her the envelope. As soon as he turns to run, I crank the car to pick him up. He dashes

*back to the car and we're able to leave without anyone
giving us a second look. Now, I just have to wait. She'll
come home, she has to.*

****

Jane

I felt Jay's arms wrap tightly around me as I took a
deep breath. He held me to his chest and I slowly
released my clenched fists then wrapped my arms around
his waist. With my ear to his chest, I could hear his heart
beating and the sound soothed me. I watched as Justin
picked up the paper Jay had dropped onto the table and
he quickly scanned it.

"This is a request for a DNA test that appears to be
done through a lawyer and not the court. Jane, you don't

have to respond unless it's court ordered," Justin said studying it closely. His brows furrowed in confusion. "Jane, I think this letter is a fake."

I lifted my head and held out my hand. "What do you mean? Let me see."

We huddled around the paper as Justin pointed out the letterhead. "The letter says to contact their office by phone and gives a number that appears to be a cell phone number. Also, this lawyer must have a crappy office because I happen to know that this address is to a building that's under construction. There are no tenants in it, only construction workers."

At the mention of construction workers, it hit me. "Mark." I looked up at Jay and saw confusion on his face. "The guy who gave me the paper was Mark. He was a buddy of Tyler's from the construction company but he looks different now."

Jay's jaw tensed. "What kind of crazy game is he playing?" He said taking the paper to look it over more closely. "Well, he should have used spellcheck too because he misspelled attorney." He moved to ball up the paper but stopped short. "This is evidence to go along with all the other crap he's been pulling." He walked over to his office and I saw him pull out a folder and place the letter inside. He sat down and started typing on his computer.

Callie shook her head. "Jane, this is getting way out of hand. He's got to be using or drinking again to be this irrational. First the break-in and now this?"

Justin put his arm around my shoulders. "Jane, you have the advantage of knowing this letter is a fake. He's probably patting himself on the back thinking you'll fall for it and will come running back to him begging for him to drop this."

I looked at Justin with curiosity. "What are you getting at?"

"You can beat Tyler at his own game. Everything he's done or will do will end up hurting him in the long run, if he ever gets this into court," he said nodding with a mischievous grin. "I say we give him enough rope and he'll end up hanging himself."

Jay joined us with a satisfied look on his face. "I did a reverse phone lookup on this "lawyer's" phone number and it comes back to Mark Gibson. I got his address too. What have I missed?"

Justin filled him in as I walked over to Jolene who was happily singing along with her movie. I could feel the anger leaving me as I watched her. She was the love of my life and no one was going to take her away from me. I kissed her on the top of the head and she looked up at me with those deep blue eyes and puckered up. I gave her a kiss and she smiled. My heart melted. I ruffled her hair and whispered, "I love you, baby."

As I walked back across the office, I saw my true family looking back at me. I took Jay's hand feeling its strength which gave me resolve. Smiling, I said, "What do I have to do?"

****

Jay

Jane's expression had changed from the time she walked away until she came back to us. She seemed strengthened and I could only guess she was thinking of Sweet Pea. I reached out my hand to her and felt her tiny hand slip into mine. I wanted to kiss her and make this all go away but I knew that wasn't going to happen. I pulled her close and tucked her head under my chin as I ran my hands up and down her back. She looked up at me with those deep blue eyes and my heart did a flip. She had that effect on me and I doubted it would ever go away.

Remembering the first day I saw her, really saw her, I had to smile. She'd been around the office and I'd been a little stuck up, I guess, but I never really looked at her. Callie had always been on my mind since I'd met her when she joined the firm. Jane was her assistant and I'd barely given her a second look the day I got enough courage to ask Callie to dinner. The dinner had been a disaster but the blessing happened the next day when I went to check on Callie who had left our dinner date with an upset stomach.

I'd never forget it. She'd come into the office to warn Callie about Matt Cooper or the "weasel" as they called him lurking around the office. As luck would have it, I ended up staying with her while Callie lured him away from the office. She'd left me with beautiful blue-eyed Jane and I found myself wanting to know more. Before she'd left us, Callie had informed me that Jane was going to be let go from her job because of the merger and I'd been livid. She'd also informed me that Jane was a single mom and this was going to be devastating to her and her young daughter. Her story pulled at my heartstrings as I thought about my own mother who'd had to raise me by herself after my father left us to follow his new love, gambling. We sat together and talked and I immediately was drawn to her frankness and strength. I didn't hesitate to ask her to dinner making sure to include her daughter so she'd feel more comfortable. I was so affected by her job situation that I'd excused myself and went straight to Mr. Mathewson's office. His secretary stalled me long enough for a redhead, who I later learned was Ashley, to come out of his office slightly disheveled and looking rather smug. I was shown into his office and I immediately questioned the new policy with Jane and her little girl foremost in my mind. He'd point blank told me that the policies were in stone and directed by the new owner. I felt compelled to quit and did so. I told him I was not going to be a part of that kind of firm and I told him I'd begin the paperwork to dissolve my partnership. I left his office abruptly mainly because I wanted to see those exquisite blue eyes again as soon as possible. When I knocked on Callie's door and opened it, I found my eyes drawn to the most perfect bottom I'd ever seen. When I saw Jane hiding behind the couch I knew that there was an attraction there, one I wasn't going to deny. Every day since, I'd fallen more in love with her and despite all the obstacles, we'd gotten engaged and I planned on spending the rest of my life making her happy.

Justin and I had come up with a plan to catch Tyler off guard. We had to keep him thinking that his "paperwork" had fooled us and that Jane was on the defensive. In reality, she would be using his ignorance to her advantage. I really didn't want her to have any more contact with him but if the end result was his being out of our lives, I was all in.

Jolene got up from the desk where she'd been watching her movie and skipped over to where we were standing. "Daddy, I want a hug, too. Can I have a hug, too?"

My heart melted as I looked down into those big blue eyes. I let Jane go and scooped Jolene up between us. She wrapped one arm around each of us and we both hugged her tightly. I loved this feeling, especially when she called me daddy. Justin put his arm around Callie and placed his hand on her blossoming belly. At that moment, it hit me how much I would love to be sharing that same thing with Jane. I wanted us to get married and have a family together as soon as possible but I wasn't going to push her until she was ready to do it. As if reading my mind, she squeezed my shoulder and I saw she was watching them closely like I was. I kissed her forehead and then felt Jolene do the same to me. These girls had my heart wrapped up tight. Jane picked up the piece of paper and her cell phone. "So, what do I need to tell him?" She asked Justin and me.

Justin grabbed a piece of paper and started writing some information down. I put Jolene back down and watched as she ran back over to her movie. "Okay, this is what we're going to do. You'll call the fake attorney and tell him that instead of doing the DNA through their office, you're going to petition the court for the test and after that, you're going to go for full custody and back child support."

Jane looked at Justin, eyes wide. "What's he going to do when I say that? Won't he be mad and try something else?"

I pulled her in close for a hug. "I dare him to try anything else," I said firmly. "He'll probably turn tail and run thinking he'll be responsible for support especially since he hasn't got any money." I was so thankful Jane and Jolene were staying with me at my house now because that low life wouldn't be able to find them.

With shaking hands, Jane dialed the number and pressed send on her phone as she studied the "script". Putting it on speakerphone, we listened as it connected. "Yo! Ahem, I mean…Smith Lawyer's office."

Jane spoke softly. "Mr. Smith? This is Jane Carter. I'm calling about the paperwork that I was served with this morning."

"Uh, yeah, Miss Carter. I guess you want to go ahead and contact the BNA testing place we wrote down in the letter." It was obvious he was not the sharpest crayon in the box.

Jane stifled a giggle. "Don't you mean DNA?"

He cleared his throat. "Ahem, oh yes, of course. DNA, that's what I meant."

Jane's voice grew strong. "Actually, I have gone to the courthouse since receiving your paperwork and have petitioned the court for paternity testing and then filed for full custody with child support back-dating for four years." We could hear nothing but silence. "Mr. Smith? Are you still there?"

A moment later we heard, "I'm gonna have to call you back. I gotta make a phone call." The call disconnected.

I took a deep breath, "Well, I think we've got him freaking out right now. He's probably calling Tyler to ask what to do next." I wrapped my arm around Jane and gave her a soft kiss. "I'm so proud of you, baby," I whispered in her ear. She gave me a smile that melted my heart. "I couldn't have done this without all of your support," she said looking at each of us. "I love you guys." At that moment, her phone rang. "Hello?"

"Miss Carter? This is Mr. Smith, lawyer. Um, I called my client Tyler and he said that ain't gonna work." He sounded really nervous.

Jane smiled. "Excuse me? What do you mean? He really has no say in this. This is the court's decree and he's gonna have to make it work."

He mumbled a curse and then said, "We'll have to get back with you."

I watched Jane bite her lip, take a deep breath and say the one thing she knew would get a reaction. "My fiancé and I will be waiting to hear from you."

There was complete silence. Finally, we heard the call disconnect again.

Jane looked at me and gave me a weak smile. "I had to tell him. This delusion he has about us getting back together has to end."

"I agree, but that was your call to make," I said wrapping her back in my arms. "Well, all we can do now is wait for his next move."

Justin nodded in agreement as Callie spoke, "I just hope he doesn't do anything stupid."

Chapter 1

Two weeks later…

Callie

Tyler's stunt had completely thrown everyone into alert mode. Jane was noticeably tense and I could see it was wearing on her. I think the not knowing was the worst. Jay and Justin had gone over to her apartment and moved the rest of her things out and she and Jolene were now living at Jay's. The security of being there did ease her mind some but when she had to leave the house for anything, it was obvious she was on pins and needles the whole time. I tried to get her mind off of it by taking her to the spa for a girl's day. Since I was about 4 weeks from my due date, I was getting more and more uncomfortable and I figured a massage would help. Jane and I arrived at the spa and were given soft fluffy robes and flip flops to slip into. After getting comfy, we went into the lounge where they provided us with fresh fruit and smoothies.

"So, tell me. How are you holding up?" I asked after I plopped down on a soft couch. Jane tucked her leg underneath her as she sat next to me. Being super-pregnant, I was secretly jealous she could do that. She turned to face me and gave me a weak smile.

Taking a deep breath and blowing it out she said, "It's been so weird that I haven't heard a word from Tyler since that day with the fake lawyer. I keep thinking he's plotting something because I know he won't just let it go. I've been a wreck and I don't know what I would've done without Jay. He's everything I could've asked for and more. He's very protective of Jolene and I and he insisted on taking Jolene today so I'd be able to relax knowing she was safe."

"Well, I know Jay loves you and Jolene very much. It's written all over his face when he sees you. You'd think he'd won the lottery." I poked her in the arm to emphasize my point. "You deserve the fairytale Jane."

She smiled sadly. "I would love to be as positive as you are Callie, but I've got Tyler in the mix and he's not going to be satisfied until he's either gotten Jolene and I back or ruined my life. Either way, it's a no-win situation."

We were interrupted by our massage therapists calling us back for our sessions. I'd scheduled the couple's package for us with the pregnant lady modification because I really wanted the strawberries dipped in chocolate and Jane was willing to sacrifice and take my share of the champagne. Within a few minutes, I could tell she was getting a buzz because she started talking about random stuff.

"I saw the cutest puppy video on spacebook this morning," she said before breaking out in laughter.

"Spacebook? Really?" I couldn't help but laugh with her.

"Spacebook, Facepage…whatever," she chuckled before snorting.

I was on my side getting my massage so I looked up at my massage therapist, Brandi. "Do you get this a lot?"

She replied very seriously, "Well, not with the pregnant massage." Jane burst out laughing even harder at that. I rolled my eyes. "I'm sure you don't. I meant the stupidity from the champagne buzz that my friend apparently has."

"Oh yes, we get that a lot. At least you aren't a married couple and the drunken husband is trying to grab us while his wife is face down on the table," she said while rubbing more oil on me.

The other massage therapist, Emily started laughing. "Yeah the other day we had a couple who were getting married and the guy, who was much older than his fiancée, started trying to grab my butt when I turned around to get the hot rocks. Let's just say I strategically placed them in certain areas so he forgot all about me." I looked over at Jane to see if she was thinking what I was thinking.

She lifted her head from the table to look at me. "The bride didn't happen to have red hair and act really bitchy, did she?" She asked with eyebrows raised.

Lowering her voice to a whisper, Brandi said, "We really shouldn't talk about clients…"

I whispered, "We won't tell, promise."

The girls exchanged another glance before I saw a slight nod between them. "Okay," Brandi continued in a hushed tone, "it started when she came in for her appointment. She was late and her fiancé had already been here long enough to chug back a couple of beers. She started in on us as soon as she got here blaming everyone but herself for being late. I was waiting for her to blame her guy but I think she's still trying to be nice to him until they get married. She knows where the money is and from what I could tell he has plenty."

Emily nodded, "Yes, he was tossing cash around giving big tips to Renee who brought him his beer. He also seemed to have a problem keeping his robe closed. When I said I was providing his service, he smirked and asked if I ever worked off the clock." Emily then motioned sticking her finger down her throat. "Really, the dude was super nerdy and I was NOT interested."

I couldn't help but ask, "Do you remember their names? They sound really familiar to me," I snickered.

Emily appeared in thought then she spoke, "You promise you won't say anything? We can really get in trouble."

I looked over at Jane who was now up on her elbow. "We promise, don't we Jane? Please, we just need to know if it's who we think it is."

Brandi spoke up, "His last name was Chase. I remember because I kept thinking of him "chasing" women around. I don't remember her name. Believe me, I've tried to forget her."

I had to speak up, "Could it have been…Ashley?" I asked innocently.

Brandi's eyes popped wide open. "YES! Ashley Battleship or something."

I snorted when I laughed. "Blankenship, maybe?"

Brandi nodded sheepishly. "Yeah, I guess it wasn't battleship…maybe that's what I think of when I think of her," she chuckled. "She kept griping at me not to get her hair extensions oily."

I cracked up. "Hair extensions! Oh my God, since when has she needed extensions?"

Brandi started laughing and said, "She had a head full of them. They were the cheap kind too, econo-weave."

Jane was laughing so hard she couldn't breathe. She held up a finger while attempting to take deep breaths but kept erupting into another fit of laughter.

"Well, she probably can't afford the good ones because she hasn't actually married him yet," I told Brandi. "She was my college roommate and I know all about her evil ways. My best friend Jane over there whacked her across the face not too long ago."

Brandi and Emily both looked over at Jane with adulation. "You whacked her?" Brandi asked in awe.

Jane recovered enough to blurt out, "Slapped the bitch hard!" She then dissolved into another fit of laughter.

"What did she do to make you slap her, besides being her wonderful self," Emily asked me, her voice dripping with sarcasm.

"She tried to steal my man and she called me fat," I said with a hurt tone.

"She tried to what? And she called a pregnant woman fat? She deserved to be slapped!" Emily said while swinging her hand as if slapping Ashley herself. "Did it feel good?" She asked Jane.

Jane nodded while catching her breath. "It felt SO good. She hurt my friend with her bitchy attitude and I'd had enough," she managed to say finally.

"What did you do after she slapped her?" Brandi asked me. I looked over at my best friend and smiling I said, "I took my bodyguard to Victoria's Secret for a shopping spree."

Both girls nodded and laughed as if shopping was the most logical thing to do after a bitch-slapping.

"Well, I for one am glad you took care of her. She really seems to have a big attitude," Emily said while finishing up Jane's massage. "I hope you ladies will come back again. We loved hanging out with you today." They helped me get up off the table and I felt a strong cramp. I'd been getting them a lot lately and every time I got one, Justin would spring into action. He'd grab my little overnight bag, throw some stuff in it and dash for the door. Naturally by this time my cramp would be over and I'd be digging in the pantry for something to eat. Last night I'd had a pretty intense one so he did his freak out routine and I ended up calling him on his cell phone to tell him that since he was already in the car to run to Taco Bell for me. He walked back upstairs opened the door and looked at me like I'd lost my mind. All I could do was laugh.

"Are you sure you're okay?" He asked looking at me with concern, "And are you absolutely sure you want Taco Bell because I'm NOT eating it this time."

Five minutes had passed and my craving had changed so I asked him to go to Krispy Kreme instead. I didn't have to ask twice. I knew that was something he loved to eat and they wouldn't go to waste.

I felt Jane touch my arm. "You okay?" She asked putting her arm around me as support.

"Yeah, just another one of those darn cramps," I said rubbing circles on my tummy. "Little Ryder isn't so little anymore and he's getting anxious to get out."

"Well, it won't be long now. How often are you going to the doctor?"

I took a deep breath to ease the pain. "Every week. I'm on the homestretch." I could feel it slowly easing off and knew it wasn't serious. "It's going away. I'll be all right." We walked to the locker room and changed back into our clothes. I had to ask something that had been bugging me. "Jane, do you think I'm fat?"

Jane's head whipped around to look at me. "Callie, haven't we already been through this before?

You are gorgeous and most definitely not fat! Has someone said something that got you upset?"

I finally couldn't keep it inside any longer. "My mom said something the other day about how she gained forty pounds when she was pregnant with me and that she's still trying to lose the baby weight. She mentioned I looked like I'd gained a few pounds myself and when I went to my doctor appointment this week, they said I'd gained a few but I don't want to have Ryder and still look like the Goodyear blimp." I felt better for sharing because it really had been bothering me.

Jane looked at me like I'd instantly grown a third head. "Are you serious? Callie, how many times do I have to tell you how wonderful you look? Your mom has always made you feel insecure and now is not the time to try to diet. Ryder needs his mommy healthy so he will be too."

I squirmed a little. "How did you know I was dieting?"

"Um, let's see. The only other reason you'd be eating lettuce and drinking water would be if you were trying out for a supermodel job. Those skinny girls are the ones who live on that kind of diet. You need good food and I'm not the only one who's noticed. I know for a fact Justin is worried about you."

I took a deep breath and sighed. "I know it's wrong but I can't help it. I've always been insecure and this has played havoc with my mind. Ashley's comments didn't help."

Jane shook her head and rolled her eyes. "Really? You're going to let the snide remarks from a back-stabbing, money-grubbing, bed-hopping, fake-hair wearing bitch bother you?"

I couldn't help but laugh. She was right. I was still letting Ashley get to me. I had a wonderful husband, awesome family and friends and a beautiful baby on the way. What was I thinking? My life was pretty darn wonderful.

"You're right. I love you, Jane. You are my compass. You always keep me pointed the right way."

We walked out to our cars, I hugged my best friend and I drove home feeling a lot better.

****

Justin

I knew she'd be home soon. I'd planned everything perfectly and the phone call from Jane let me know I had about fifteen minutes to get everything perfect. I couldn't wait for her to walk through the door and see what I'd been up to. I knew she was feeling down and I knew I needed to do something to make things better. I'd been so busy lately with the museum project that I forgot the simple things that made her happy. Sure I'd made plenty of "craving" runs to Taco Bell and they'd even gotten to know me by my voice at the late night drive thru. All I had to do was say, "Hi" and they'd start laughing and ask what she was craving now. It became a game for the employees and I'd usually hear a cheer over the intercom as one of them got her order right. Well, tonight was going to be different. I had made big plans and it was going to be a night she'd never forget.

I heard the key in the lock and I lowered the lights. Callie opened the door and I heard her call out, "Justin? Is there something wrong with the lights?" She came around the corner and stopped and stared. I'd transformed our living room into my suite at the hotel where we first met. I'd replicated everything down to the silverware on the table. Callie walked into the room with her mouth open in shock. I walked up to her, took her hand and kissed it gently. I could see tears welling up in her eyes so I spoke up, "Wow, Callie. You look absolutely incredible."

She started laughing as the tears spilled out onto her cheeks. "Well, Justin, you look…nice."

I pulled her into my arms as I whispered, "Nice is good." I kissed her softly on the cheek then moved slowly to her beautiful mouth where I placed a lingering kiss. I felt her lean into me and I held her tighter. "I love you, Callie. I wanted to show you how much our first night meant to me." I released her from my arms only to grab her hand to lead her to the table. Pulling out her chair, I let her sit down and I gently ran my hand through her hair, reliving that same moment from that night. She turned to look at me with surprise. "You know, I thought your hair was so beautiful and soft. I wanted to run my fingers through it all night long."

"I had no idea you were thinking these things," she said looking at me with sheer amazement.

"Babe, if you'd known everything I was thinking that night we would never have made it to the seminar the next day," I said waggling my eyebrows.

She snickered. "Oh you thought I was a sure thing, did you?" I saw her cheeks were flushed now.

"No, but I think you would have eventually given in to my irresistible charm and good looks. I would have enjoyed trying to convince you but I also respected you and was willing to wait." I took her hand and gently kissed the ring I placed on her finger just a few months ago. "I'm so glad I did because it was worth every moment."

She lowered her eyes then looked back up and I saw the green of her eyes had deepened. I leaned in and kissed her again, slowly and gently. I placed my hand on her tummy and felt little Ryder move and I couldn't help but smile against her mouth. "Is our little man hungry?" I said feeling a rumble in addition to his movement.

Callie smiled sheepishly, "I hate to say this, but yes. Whatever you made for dinner smells heavenly. But you've definitely got me begging for an after dinner treat."

"You've got it. Let me feed you and my hungry baby." I got up and lifted the lids off the warming dish. "We have filet mignon and salmon for the beautiful lady."

Callie's eyes grew wide. "You even cooked? Justin, this is absolutely fantastic. It smells so good and you remembered everything! I can't believe this."

Seeing her face light up made everything worthwhile. I placed a portion on each plate just like I had that night and sat down next to her. She looked down at the plate then back at me. "Are you going to feed me, Justin?" She asked with a playful grin.

"I'll do whatever you want, babe. Tonight is all about you." I cut a piece of the filet and held it out to her. I watched as her perfect lips parted and I found mine opening along with hers. She closed her lips around the steak and made a soft moan. She chewed ever so slowly and I found myself so turned on by something so simple. "Babe, you keep doing that and we won't make it to the salmon," I managed to squeak out. She smiled and wrinkled her nose at me. That was all it took. I slid my hand around her neck and pulled her in for a passionate kiss. Her lips were so soft and her breath so sweet. She slid her hands around my shoulders and up into my hair. I loved how it felt when she tangled her hands in it and lightly tugged. Breathless, I broke the kiss and stood taking her hand. I led her into the bedroom where I stopped to kiss her again. She tugged my shirt off and was about to throw it when suddenly she grabbed her stomach.

"Oh…that hurts," she said before taking a deep breath.

"You okay? Is it the baby? Do I need to get your bag?" This contraction thing was a tricky business and I had a habit of overreacting. Trying to appear calm I held on to her as she breathed through it. After a few minutes her breathing became regular again.

"It's easing off now. Wow that was a pretty intense one," she said still clutching her stomach. "That was a mood killer, huh?"

"Nothing could ever kill my desire for you babe, but obviously you need to lie down and rest. I'll bring you some dinner on a tray. No hanky panky for you tonight. You'll just have to have hot dreams about me instead," I said leading her over to the bed. Before she sat down, she stroked her hands down the front of my chest. Her eyes traveled up and met mine.

"I can't wait until I can ravage you the way I want to," she said sliding her hands around my waist and pulling me close. I wrapped my arms around her and rested my chin on the top of her head.

"Soon enough, babe. Soon enough."

Chapter 2

Tyler

I can't stand this waiting. How long will it be before she calls me to come back? It's been a month and I've been patiently waiting but nothing. Not a word. The only thing that keeps me here is the chance that she'll call. I had to move out of the decent hotel I was in and now I'm in a dump where they only change the sheets if you check out for good. The only thing that helps me pass the time is my trusty friend, the bottle. I've started drinking the cheapest stuff they make but as long as it keeps me numb, I don't care. I've decided I can't wait anymore. It may be the middle of the night but I'm going to go to her office, wait for her to get there and plead with her to come with me. I know she loves me. She loved me once and we had a future planned. I know I screwed up but she has to see she still loves me...she has to. I'm going to see her today. I get into my car and have a hard time putting the key in the ignition. Everything is fuzzy but I'm not that drunk, I've been drunker. I start to buckle my seat belt but I can't get it to click and it starts to tick me off so I leave it undone. I pull out of the parking lot running over the curb when I turn onto the main road.   My cell phone rings…it could be Jane! I look down to check and look back up right before the car hits the tree and I'm swallowed by the darkness.

****

Jane

I woke up in the middle of the night having a terrible nightmare. Jay wrapped his arms around me and kissed my cheek and I finally started to relax. He asked me what it was about and I couldn't for the life of me remember. He told me it was probably from not knowing what was going to happen next and he was probably right. It was eerie opening the door every morning wondering if Tyler had found us again like he had before.

It had been a month since I'd made that phone call to fake lawyer Mark and we hadn't heard a word from Tyler since. Jay was always very cautious any time we left the house and we had Jolene with us constantly. She didn't seem to be aware of anything unusual which was a blessing because I really didn't know what to tell her. Jay and I had decided that it was best not to tell her who he really was until we absolutely had to. We knew if Tyler called our bluff and really went to court then we would have to do it. I'd gotten an attorney who was going to handle the case if it got that far.

I got up out of bed to get a drink of water. I padded to our bathroom, ran some water into a glass and gulped it down. I decided to check on Jolene. She was fast asleep in her princess bed with Rapunzel tucked under her arm. I pulled the covers back over her, tucking in her leg which she'd kicked out. She murmured and rolled over, never waking up. I made my way back to the bedroom and crawled back under the covers. Jay instantly wrapped his arm around me and pulled me back to him. His warm breath on the back of my neck had always soothed me and I felt myself slowly relax.

Light creeping through the blinds woke me and I slowly opened my eyes to see Jolene standing by the bed. "What's up, pumpkin?" I whispered.

"Mama, your phone was ringing and it woke me up," she whispered back. "I brought it for you." She handed me the phone and crawled up onto the bed. Jay raised his head and saw her trying to get between us so he scooted over and grabbed her pulling her up the bed. "Good morning, Daddy," she giggled. "You have porkopine hair again."

He rolled over onto his back and ran his hands through his hair making it stand even taller. "Is this better?" He asked seriously. "Is it flatter now?"

Jolene dissolved into a fit of giggles. "NO! You made your hair higher! Daddy stop! You're gonna make me snort."

I watched them together and loved every moment. Jay was being an awesome father to her and would be to our own children one day. I looked at the phone in my hand and realized I'd better check to see who called this early in the morning. I pulled up the missed calls and saw a number I had marked "Fake lawyer" just in case he called again. He had left a voicemail. I gasped and looked up to see Jay and Jolene watching me. "Is everything okay," Jay asked with concern.

I threw back the covers and got out of bed. "I don't know. I need to listen to this in private," I said nodding my head slightly to Jolene. Jay got the message and threw back the covers.

"Let's go get some breakfast started, Sweet Pea," he said, picking her up off the bed and throwing her over his shoulder. She started giggling and they left the room with Jolene waving back at me.

My hands were trembling as I started the voicemail. It was Mark.

"Uh, hey. This is Mark, Tyler's friend…um…hell…I don't know what to say…um…Tyler's been in a wreck. I got the call this morning from a buddy of ours who's an EMT. They took Tyler to Mission Hospital and he's in critical condition. It's pretty bad. Hey, I know what we did was pretty low but I hope you'll believe me and call me back."

I was standing there staring at the phone when Jay came back in the bedroom. "You okay, baby?"

I felt so confused. It didn't seem real. "Tyler's friend Mark just called and said Tyler's been in an accident and he's in critical condition. You don't think they're messing with me, do you?"

Jay looked at me with concern. "Jane, I'll call the hospital and verify he's there." He took the phone and called Mission Hospital. "Admissions, please," he said still watching me. "Yes, I was wondering if you could tell me if a patient has been admitted. Yes, Tyler Simpson. I'll hold." He put his arm around my shoulders and pulled me in close. I instinctively wrapped my arms around his waist and lay my head on his chest. "Yes, ma'am…Tyler Simpson. No, I'm not family. Well, he and my fiancée have a child together. Right…okay thank you." He disconnected the phone and looked at me. "It's true…Tyler's in the hospital and in intensive care. He's in critical condition and they've got him on life support." My mouth gaped open. I took a deep breath as I felt tears trickling down my face. "I don't hate him, Jay. I don't want him to die."

Jay held me close. "I know, baby. You still care about the man he used to be…the man he could have been." He stroked my hair with his hand and let me cry.

****

Jay

It was breaking my heart to see her this way. Tyler may not be worth much in my eyes but he was Jolene's father. He didn't deserve to die. He was still a young man with a long life ahead and I could only pray he would make it out of this alive to have some happiness. I heard a tiny knock at the door and saw Jolene standing there. "Daddy? Is Mama ok?"

"Sure she is, Sweet Pea. Mama just had some bad news and it made her cry but she's going to be okay." Tentatively she walked into the bedroom to come stand beside me. I put my hand out and she slid her little hand in mine. Jane finally realized she was there and looked down at her as she wiped her tears away.

"Jolene…someone I know was in an accident and he's in the hospital. He's very sick and I'm worried about him. I'll be going to the hospital to see him so I'm going to drop you at daycare while Daddy and I go." When she said the last part about both of us going, I felt relieved that she wanted me there and that she wouldn't be going alone.

Jolene looked up at us and said, "I'll pray to Jesus for your friend." My heart just melted. I leaned down and picked her up to put her between us. She hung on our shoulders and gave us each a kiss on the cheek. I put her back down and figured we needed to give Jane a few minutes alone so I looked at Jolene and said, "Race you to get ready. Winner gets to go to Chuck E. Cheese."

Jolene ran squealing from the room and I nonchalantly walked over to my closet. Jane watched me closely as I slid my shirts back until I found the green one she liked so much. I studied the ties and found the one that matched and laid them all out on the bed. "You aren't even trying to win, are you?" She said shaking her head with the hint of a smile. "You're getting so good at this."

Looking at her face I knew she was just barely holding it together. She still cared about Tyler no matter how badly he'd treated her. He just didn't hold the same place in her heart that he used to. They had a child together and that was a bond that was pretty strong. I gave her a big smile. "I hope so! I've watched the best mother in the world in action. I'm just trying to be worthy."

She walked over to me and wrapped her arms around me. I took a deep breath and caught the hint of the vanilla lotion she used religiously every night before bed. "You are so worthy and I love you so much. Thank you for being so understanding about my needing to see Tyler."

I backed away slightly and lifted her chin to look into those gorgeous blue eyes. "I love you and will support whatever you need to do," I said before gently kissing her.

"I'm done!" Jolene squealed as she ran into the room. "Daddy, you haven't even got started yet! Mama, can you do my hair?"

Jane pulled away but not before giving me a quick kiss. "Sure baby, let me get your brush." As she left to get it, I went into the bathroom and got ready. When I came back out a few minutes later, Jolene's mass of curls was tamed. I volunteered to take Jolene to daycare to let Jane get ready and told her I'd be back in a few minutes. She nodded absently as she was obviously distracted. I took Jolene by the hand and we headed out. When we got to the car, I opened the door to put Jolene in. She started to climb in and she looked at me very seriously. "Daddy, is Mama's friend gonna die?"

I was floored. "Wow, Sweet Pea. Where did that come from?" I helped her in and buckled her in.

"I saw it in my movie. Nemo's mama died and his daddy had to take care of him. Simba's daddy died in his movie and his mama had to take care of him. I know that people die when they get sick or hurt so I just wondered." She picked up her Leapster and started playing with it like what she'd said was no big deal.

I got in and after a moment said, "Sweet Pea, I think we need to just pray really hard that he doesn't die, okay?"

She nodded without looking up, "Okay, Daddy. I'll pray."

Chapter 3

Callie

I got the call from Jane about Tyler's accident and yelled for Justin. He came running in and headed for the closet where my bag was and I had to stop him. "Justin, it's not time for the baby." His expression showed relief but quickly changed as I continued, "Jane just called to tell us that Tyler's in the hospital. He's been in a wreck and is in critical condition. She's headed there now."

"I know you want to go…are you up to it?" He asked while changing his shirt.

"Absolutely, Jane needs me." I grabbed the keys and my phone. "Let's go."

We drove to the hospital and saw Jay's car as we pulled into the parking lot. We didn't know where they were so we stopped at information to find out where ICU was and were directed to the fifth floor Trauma ICU. We couldn't go back in to the unit but I could see Jane leaning against the wall as Jay spoke with someone who appeared to be a nurse. Jane saw me through the doors and ran down the hall. As she came through the doors, I opened my arms to hug her. She'd been crying and I reached over to grab a tissue from the box in the waiting room. I handed her the tissue then hugged her tightly. Justin put his arms around both of us and we stood like that for a moment before we noticed Jay was headed down the hall toward us.

In a hushed tone he gave us the update, "He's still critical. The doctors have him in a medically induced coma right now. He's had some pretty serious brain trauma and they are trying to keep him stable." He reached out and pulled Jane to him.

Justin spoke up, "I'll go get us some coffee. We will probably be here a while." Jay and I walked Jane over to the waiting area where we sat on a big couch. There were others in the waiting area obviously waiting for word on their loved ones and I could feel their anxiety coming off them in waves. Jane was trembling and I held her hands trying to comfort her but there really wasn't anything more I could do except be there as her friend. Jay sat on the other side of her and was rubbing her back gently. Justin came back into the room with two trays of coffees. He set one in front of us and then offered the other to the woman and man sitting with us. They were so surprised but thankful. My heart swelled with love watching him comfort them. He glanced up at me and smiled and I wrinkled my nose at him and smiled. He gave me a wink and walked over to sit beside me. Jane looked around as if in a daze.

"The police talked to me when I got here. They said they found evidence he was drunk when he hit the tree." She threw her head back and took a deep breath. "I feel so bad. This is all because of me," she said wiping her eyes.

Jay shook his head. "Jane, you didn't cause this. Tyler's a grown man and if he chose to drink and drive then he's the one who is responsible for where he is now."

Jane sniffled, "I know but I still feel guilty. That's Jolene's father in there and she doesn't even know it." I saw Jay stiffen and I knew what he was thinking so I caught his eye and shook my head. He relaxed and I knew he'd gotten the message. Jane was going through a lot of emotions right now and I knew she didn't realize it would hurt his feelings.

A few minutes later, a doctor came in and Jane immediately tensed up but he walked over to the other family and in a hushed tone gave them an update. The woman began to wail as it was obviously bad news. "No, not my baby! He was only 18! Please no!" She threw her head onto her husband's shoulder and he bit his lip trying to control his feelings for her sake. I felt such a rush of emotion and before I knew it, tears were streaming down my cheeks. Justin grabbed a tissue and dabbed them for me. The doctor escorted them out and I saw Jane's face lose its color.

"What if they come in here and tell us Tyler's dead? What am I going to do?" She said looking around at each of us. Jay wrapped his arm around her.

"Jane, you have to just pray he'll be okay. We'll deal with that possibility if it happens," he said.

We all sat there in silence watching the television which was set on a news channel. We'd been holding vigil for about three hours when the doctor came in and this time we knew it was about Tyler. Jane stood up as the doctor walked over. "Miss Carter? I'm Doctor Ross. I'm in charge of Mr. Simpson's case. I understand you're not blood family but are the mother of his child?" Jane nodded as the doctor continued. "We've been unable to reach any family for Mr. Simpson, is he without family?"

Jane nodded, "His parents both passed away from cancer several years ago and he doesn't have any brothers or sisters. I think his only living relative is his aunt but she lives in Bermuda."

The doctor nodded, "Well, I think that qualifies you to know his condition. We can step somewhere private to discuss this, if you'd like," he said glancing at us.

"These people are my family and I'd like them to hear this with me, Doctor Ross," she said holding Jay's hand.

"Very well, Mr. Simpson suffered a traumatic brain injury but at this stage we can't determine how debilitating it will be. He's in a medically induced coma and we're monitoring the swelling in his brain. Once the swelling goes down, we'll ease him out of the coma and assess the permanent effects then."

Jane placed her hand on the doctor's arm and asked, "Is he going to die?"

"Honestly, Miss Carter…I can't answer that right now. Just keep him in your prayers and let us handle his care. He's getting the best he can get here at Mission Hospital."

"Can I see him?" She asked softly.

"We'll let you in but he's attached to wires and machines so you won't be able to touch him. You can only stay for a few minutes. I'll get a nurse to take you in." He took Jane by the elbow and walked her out. Jay was right behind her but the doctor stopped him. "I'm sorry sir, only Miss Carter right now." Jay nodded and reluctantly backed toward us. Jane turned, gave us a weak smile and walked down the hall to Tyler's room.

Jane

I hated leaving Jay behind but the doctor made it clear I had to go in alone. As I entered the door I could hear strange noises and I felt tingles all over as if I might faint. I steadied myself by holding onto the door frame as the nurse beckoned me in. I walked over to the bed and saw Tyler, his face wrapped up in bandages, his arms strapped down with IV lines trailing up to bags of fluid. He had a tube inserted in his mouth which was helping him breathe. The only sounds were the beeping of the heart monitor and the whoosh of the ventilator. The nurse gestured to a chair and I sat down, my eyes taking in everything. He'd apparently broken his nose because he had a bandage across the bridge and he had purple around his eyes from the bruising. A collar was placed around his neck and his right arm was in a cast. I noticed that he had bandages wrapped around his ribcage and tubes were snaking out of that area as well. I watched as his chest rose and fell with each puff of the machine. The nurse adjusted some settings on the machines and left me alone.

I sat there and finally had to speak. "Tyler, I don't know if you can hear me but I want you to know, I'm here. It's me, Jane." I shifted in the chair and scooted a bit closer, mindful of the machines around the bed. "No matter what you've done, Tyler, I still do care about you. I wonder every day where everything went wrong for us and it all comes back to I wasn't number one in your life. When we first met that day in school, I thought I was dreaming when my friend Jennifer told me you asked about me. She and I were walking back from the gym where I'd been secretly watching you working out with the football team and she said, 'Tyler's interested in you but he's nervous about talking to you.' I remember thinking, 'He's nervous? How could he be nervous? He's gorgeous!' The next day, I remember walking out of my 4th period class and you were standing by my locker. I walked up and somehow got the nerve to say, 'Hey, I heard you wanted to talk to me!' and you smiled and said, 'I'd like to walk you to class if you don't mind.' We walked and talked and I didn't want it to end. You said you'd meet me at the stairs and when I got out of class I rushed down to the landing, you were waiting. We talked through lunch. When I got home from school you called me and we talked for hours. You were such a great listener and I felt I could tell you anything. You listened when I talked about my mom and dad and how strict they were and I knew you were always going to be on my side. When we graduated and you wanted to move you convinced me that I needed to be with you and I walked away from my family without a look back."

I stopped to swallow back a sob that was threatening to escape and I took a deep breath before continuing. "I loved you with every breath I had, Tyler and I wanted us to be together forever." I felt a tear roll down my cheek. "You changed and I didn't want to see it at first. You never had time for me and it became less and less. I know you have a good heart but you got wrapped up in the wrong crowd and left me behind. You didn't even give Jolene a chance when you walked out…she's the innocent one in all of this." I saw the nurse coming in the door. "Tyler, I just want you to know, I love Jay and nothing is going to change that. You need to live your life in the present and future, not the past. If you can hear me, let me go." I stood and gently touched his hand. I walked two steps and felt lightheaded again. I made my way to the waiting room where I fell into Jay's strong arms.

"Jane, are you okay?" Jay asked looking at me closely.

"He looks terrible. After seeing the condition he's in, I'm surprised he's alive," I said shakily.

Callie and Justin both embraced me and Callie spoke, "Jane, you can't stay here waiting. I'm sure the hospital will keep you updated. There's nothing more you can do until his condition changes." I knew she was right.

Jay gathered my things and spoke to the nurse giving her our contact information. We all walked out together and Jay and I got in his car to head home. We rode home in silence but I could see Jay glancing at me periodically. Jolene had a few hours left at daycare so we would have some time alone. I felt so pent up, so wired. I walked in the house, threw my purse down and whipped around to stand face to face with Jay. His eyes showed his confusion but I didn't say a word. I wanted him…now. I ran my hands through his hair and feverishly kissed him. He returned the kiss tentatively at first then became bolder. Breathless, he broke the kiss. "What are you doing, Jane?" He whispered.

"I need you, I need this. Please, Jay," I begged. I started to unbutton his shirt but he stopped me. I stared at my hands.

"Is this because of Tyler? Please don't make this about him," he said trying to catch my gaze. I looked up at him and felt the tears welling up. I shook my head and took a deep breath.

"It's not about Tyler, it's about loving you and needing to be close and feel you connected with me. I don't want to ever lose you, ever."

He nodded, his eyes searching mine. In one movement, he scooped me up and carried me into our bedroom. He gently placed me on the bed, his eyes never leaving mine. I started to pull off my shirt and he stopped me. "Jane, you need this, but this is to be savored and enjoyed." He lay down beside me and gently touched the bare skin of my midriff. He brushed his lips along my jawline and I felt tingles throughout my body. He cupped my neck and tilted my head to feather kisses along the side of my neck. "I love you," he whispered and I felt a tear trickle from my eye.

"I love you, too…so much," I said, my heart almost exploding with the emotions I was feeling. He wrapped his arms around me and his mouth claimed mine. I tangled my hands in his hair returning his passionate kiss with fervor. Jay broke away breathless. "Your mouth is so soft, I can never get enough." I felt my body kick into overdrive. My heart was thundering in my chest. When he kissed me again, he let loose a deep growl that only fueled my intensity. My hands moved to unbutton his shirt and I tugged it from him. His voice was husky when he spoke, "Jane, I want you." He looked into my eyes and saw the desire, saw the need. I touched his chest tracing the contours of his muscles, really focusing on his needs as well as my own. He nipped at my neck as I stroked the hair on his chest. He tugged at my shirt lifting it from me completely and then worshipped my bare skin. "You are so beautiful," he said softly, his eyes devouring my body.

I cupped his face with my fingers then trailed them down to his strong jawline. Touching his lips with the tip of my finger, I felt his tongue dart out sending tingles throughout my body. I moved in to kiss him again and lightly nipped his lip with my teeth making him growl again. I was trembling with anticipation as he slid off the rest of my clothes. He pulled my naked body against him, his warm hands spanning my bare back. I moved my hands down his chest to his jeans where I fumbled with the button. He pulled away, stood up and with a sexy smile, unbuttoned and slipped them off. He joined me back on the bed and my hands ran up and down his muscular back and shoulders. He kissed me passionately as he wrapped his arms around me, our bodies fitting together like pieces in a puzzle. There were no words, only the sound of gentle murmurs and sighs. I closed my eyes, focusing on every sensation, every touch. I heard Jay whisper, "Please look at me." As my eyes fluttered open, I locked on to Jay's searing gaze. "I love you, Jane," he whispered. I captured his mouth with mine as we rode the waves of ecstasy and as I shattered, I cried out his name against his shoulder. Breathless, we lay with our legs tangled together, neither of us wanting to lose the moment. We stayed wrapped in each other's arms until the ringing of my phone brought us back to reality. It was the hospital calling. Tyler was improving.

Chapter 4

Justin

Callie started complaining about her Braxton Hicks contractions right after we got home from the hospital. I wanted to take her back right away but she insisted it would be okay. I got her comfortably in bed to rest and decided to do something special for her. We'd already cleaned out the junk room and bought the crib but with everything going on, we hadn't started actually putting it together. I put on some old clothes, grabbed the drop cloths and got to work. Callie had chosen a soft blue for the wall color and she'd had an awesome idea to put letters and numbers on the wall in a glaze. I popped open the paint can and started rolling away and in no time, I had the walls finished. I took a break to check on Callie and seeing she was out cold, I gave her a kiss on the forehead and went back to assemble the crib. I was just tightening the last bolt when I heard the phone ring. I checked and saw it was Jay.

"What's up, Jay?" I said quietly so I didn't disturb Callie.

"We just heard from the hospital. They've upgraded Tyler from critical to serious condition. From what I understand, it won't be long before they wake him up and take him off the vent."

"Do you need us to do anything?"

"No man, thanks. Jane and I are going to pick up Jolene and just wait for updates. Thank you again for being there for Jane. She appreciates everything you both have done. I'll call you later." I hung up and looked in on Callie again. She seemed to be restless but asleep so I went back to work. I finished painting and was just getting ready to put the crib against the wall when I had a great idea. I painted Ryder on the wall and slid the crib under it. I was just putting the furniture in place when I heard a noise down the hallway.

"Justin, babe? Where are you?" Callie called out. I walked out of the bedroom and found her headed my way. "What are you up to?" She asked

"Close your eyes. I have a surprise," I said taking her hand.

"Another one? I don't know if I can handle many more of your awesome surprises," she said smiling. I led her down to the bedroom making sure she was keeping her eyes tightly shut. I put her in front of me at the door and turned the knob. As the door swung open, I nudged her forward and put my hands over her eyes.

"Ready?" I whispered in her ear.

"Yes," she said softly. I pulled my hands away and heard her gasp. "JUSTIN!" She cried. "It's beautiful! How did you do all this?" I heard a hitch in her breath and looked around to see her face scrunched up as she tried not to cry.

I turned her around to face me. "Babe, I wanted to make this beautiful for you and Ryder. Is it what you wanted? Please say yes," I said with a smile.

Through her tears, she nodded. "It's perfect, just like you. I love you." She brushed the hair out of my eyes and stood on her toes to kiss me softly. I wrapped my arms around her and held her against my chest. She turned slightly to get closer and I placed my hand on her tummy. I felt Ryder move against my hand and my heart swelled with love. I couldn't wait to meet our little man and see how beautiful he would be.

"I love you too, babe," I whispered. "I hope little Ryder has his mom's good looks and beautiful soul." I gently kissed her. Her eyes tilted up to look at me and I saw those beautiful green eyes brimming with tears. One single tear slipped out and rolled down her cheek. I cupped her face and wiped the tear away with my thumb. I kissed where it had been then feathered kisses over to her full bottom lip which was quivering now as she tried to hold back her tears. I felt her sigh against my mouth and then return the kiss, slowly then more passionately. I opened my eyes to see hers hooded with desire. I took her by the hand and led her to our bedroom. The time was right to quench the desire that had been building for so long.

****

Jay

Anticipating Jane would be wound up tight with worry about Tyler, I decided it was best for us to work from home the next day. We dropped Jolene off at daycare because they were having a special program at the center and we thought it would be best to keep her schedule as routine as possible. We worked most of the morning and got a lot accomplished on some new proposals for a restaurant as well as the renovation of a hotel. Jane was constantly looking at her phone and I could tell she was anxious but she never said a word. When it was time to pick up Jolene, I told Jane to stay at the house while I went to pick her up. She came bounding out of her classroom with her new teacher, Miss Torri. Jolene had adapted well to being at the new daycare and the staff had been briefed about our situation. Tyler wouldn't be a threat for a while but we still appreciated their understanding and extra attention.

"Daddy! I drew you a picture!" She said holding up a piece of construction paper.

I looked at it and saw her stick-figure representation of the three of us. I had hair sticking straight up and I started to laugh. "Sweet Pea, my hair doesn't always stick up like that!" I said as she started to giggle.

She snorted and said, "But Daddy, I like it best this way!"

I picked her up and whispered, "Well, then fix it for me then." She took her hand and rubbed it all through my hair making it stand up just like it did in her picture. Miss Torri was in hysterics laughing at us and I grinned sheepishly. "She's my stylist. I can't go wrong." My phone rang and I quickly answered it thinking it might be Jane with news.

"Jay Anderson," I said putting Jolene down to take her by the hand.

"Jay, this is Tristan O'Neal. I'm Mr. Davenport's personal assistant. I hate to bother you this late in the afternoon but there's a problem and I was wondering if I could run over to your office to clear it up before it slows up the construction."

I covered the phone and looked down at Jolene. I whispered, "Do you want to go with me to work for a few minutes?" Her face lit up and she nodded vigorously. I went back to the call, "Ok, I'll be there in about ten minutes."

I called Jane on the way to the office to tell her where we were going and she said she hadn't heard any more about Tyler. We pulled up in front of the office and saw a tall blonde man standing in the parking lot. I assumed it was Tristan but since I'd never actually met him, only spoken with him on the phone, I wasn't sure. We climbed from the car and smiling, he walked over to us.

"Jay? I'm Tristan. Nice to finally meet you," he said extending his hand for a shake.

"Same here. Tristan, this is Jolene." Tristan knelt down and extended his hand to her to shake hers as well.

"Hi, Miss Jolene. My name is Tristan."

She looked at him and smiled, "I like that name. You have pretty hair." She looked up at me and grinned, "He has his hair in a ponytail like me."

Tristan laughed, "Yes, I do. I like my hair a little longer so I wear it pulled back so my boss doesn't get too upset. Do you like it?"

"I do! You look like a prince," she said giggling. I laughed with her.

"Well, Tristan, I believe you've got a fan," I said unlocking the office. He followed me in and I turned on the lights. "We weren't in the office today because we had some bad news yesterday morning. A friend of Jane's was hurt in an accident so we were up at the hospital most of the day and were awaiting updates today."

"Well, I wish them a speedy recovery. My dad's in the hospital back home and I know how stressful that can be," he said pulling out his folder with the paperwork we needed to go over. Jolene sat in my office chair watching us pull up the design on the computer. Once Tristan pointed out where the contractor was stumped I knew exactly what to tell him. We wrapped it up pretty quickly and I decided to grab some Chinese on the way home so Jane didn't have to cook. I called her and she didn't answer so I just left a message hoping that she would get it before starting dinner. Tristan thanked me for taking the time to straighten out the confusion and mentioned how nicely it was coming along and that Mr. Davenport was very pleased.

Jolene and I bundled into the car and headed to FooJo's to get the food. I tried Jane again and still got no answer. When we pulled up at the house, I saw her car was gone. I called Justin and he answered immediately.

"Jane's at the hospital. She got a call that they were going to try to wake Tyler up and take him off the vent. She said she tried to call you but didn't get an answer." I'd never heard my phone ring and then it hit me that I'd let Jolene play her game on it and we'd turned the sound down.

"Ok, thanks, man. I've got to figure out what to do now with Jolene," I said desperate to get to Jane.

"Bring her over here. We're just sitting around watching movies. Callie has her feet up and is taking it easy," he replied.

"Have you guys eaten yet? I've got Chinese food."

"We have not eaten and you can bring it on," Justin said laughing. "I actually eat that!"

I changed direction and headed downtown to drop Jolene off at Callie and Justin's. Once she was safely inside and I'd waved at Mrs. Callahan who always happened to be in the hallway when I went by, I headed to the hospital.

Chapter 5

Tyler

I hurt everywhere. The pain is so intense and it hurts to breathe. I have something down my throat and it scares me. Cold hands touch my arm and I flinch from the cold. I hear a woman's voice say, 'He's waking up,' but I can't quite open my eyes. Where am I and why can't I move? I try to move my arms but find them being restrained and I begin to panic. The voice tells me to calm down and I feel the prick of a needle and I find myself relaxing. I'm aware of smells and sounds that aren't familiar. Within moments, a male voice tells me he's a doctor and that I've been in an accident. I don't remember any of that but I do remember hearing Jane's voice. It felt like a dream but it seemed so real. He asks me to open my eyes and I do but everything is blurry at first. It takes a moment to clear and then I'm able to see the people who have been talking to me. A man stands over me in a white coat speaking to a woman in scrubs. They tell me to cough and he pulls the tube out of my throat. I'm starting to feel like I won't be able to breathe. The man tells me to take a deep breath. I gasp and panic at first until I realize it's going to be okay. I take a deep breath and try to speak but it comes out instead as a hoarse whisper, "Jane."

****

Jane

I'd wanted to tell Jay that I was going to the hospital but he didn't answer, so I left a voice mail and headed over there. I called Callie and Justin on the way and told them where I was headed and they asked if they needed to come down and I assured them I was going to be fine. I pulled into the hospital parking lot, turned off my car, took a deep breath and went in. At the door of the ICU, I rang the bell and the same nurse I'd seen yesterday waved at me and opened the door.

"How is he?" I said anxiously. Smiling, she took me by the arm and led me into his room. He was sitting up in the bed, still covered in bandages but his eyes were open and focused on me. I walked around the foot of the bed and his eyes followed me as I moved until I sat in the stiff plastic chair next to his bed. We sat like that for several minutes, the only sound was the beep of his heart monitor and the hum of the IV machines. Finally, he spoke, his voice raspy, "I dreamed of you."

I sat looking at him with confusion. He'd been in a medically induced coma. How could this be possible? "What do you mean you dreamed of me?" I questioned.

He closed his eyes and appeared to have drifted off to sleep but then he spoke again, "I dreamed you were here talking to me. You told me that you still cared about me but that you loved someone else." He kept his eyes closed as if it was too hard to say what he needed to say while looking at me. "I've been in love with you Jane almost all my life and I don't know how to do anything else."

I scooted my chair closer and placed my left hand on his arm, careful not to disturb his IV lines. He opened his eyes to look at me and I saw a single tear roll down his cheek. "Tyler, I don't know how you heard that but it's true. Jay is a good man and Jolene and I love him."

He looked down at my hand and saw the ring, my engagement ring. He took a deep breath and blew it out. "So it's official. You're gonna marry the guy. Well, I'll say this, he's got great taste in rings…and women." He chuckled a little, "I'd never be able to compete with someone like that."

"Tyler, there's no competition. I care for you and I always will but I love Jay…with all my heart," I said, my voice breaking with emotion.

He lifted his head to look straight at me. "Jane, I've been stupid. I almost killed myself with my stupidity and I'm sorry. I can't possibly take care of Jolene. Hell, I can't even take care of myself," he said softly. "All I can do with this second chance is make my life better and maybe one day, when she's older, she'll want to meet me and get to know who I am."

I felt tears spring into my eyes and I blinked them back quickly. "Tyler that would be totally up to her. She knows Jay as Daddy now and I don't want to confuse her but maybe one day, when she's older, we can tell her the truth and let her decide what she wants to do."

He nodded and laid his head back against the pillows. "If you're going to tell her the truth, then I want you to tell her the real truth." He looked away from me as if mustering the courage to tell me. "I lied about everything. I did go to rehab…for two days. I tried the meetings for my drug addiction but couldn't stick with it. I finally came to the conclusion that getting you back was the only way to make my life right," he said with a sigh.

"Tyler, none of this made sense. I know you better than you think I do. The threats, the breaking into my house…they just weren't the actions of the man I knew."

He glanced at me briefly then quickly looked away. "I'm so ashamed of that too. I should have never gone that far. I'm sorry I put you through that. Jolene didn't get hurt by any of that, did she?"

"No, thank God. We kept her away so she never saw any of it," I said softly.

I heard him take a deep breath. "I'm going to give up trying to get her. I'm going to sign papers giving up any claim to paternity. I need to tell you, the stuff from the lawyer was all fake. Mark and I made it up."

"Yeah," I nodded. "We kind of figured that out pretty quickly," I said covering my mouth to stifle a laugh.

He looked over at me and with a sheepish grin he said, "I guess it was kinda dumb on my part to let Mark help me."

"Well, he could have at least spelled attorney right," I said unable to stop my laughter.

He suddenly looked at me seriously. "Bring the papers and I'll do the right thing."

The nurse walked in at that moment and started to check his vital signs, "Mr. Simpson, there's a young lady outside who says she's your sister." Tyler and I both looked at her with confusion because Tyler didn't have a sister. "She says her name is Cailynn. Ring a bell?"

Tyler's expression reflected surprise. "Cailynn? How did she find me?" He said in disbelief.

"You know who she is, Tyler?" I asked watching him closely.

"Yes, she was my counselor in rehab. We kinda dated a few times but I sorta left without saying goodbye to come back here for you."

The nurse smiled, "Would you like me to send her in?"

"Uh, yeah, I'd like to know why she's here" he said.

I stood to leave them alone and Tyler reached out for my hand. "I'd like you to meet her."

I sat back down reluctantly and saw the door open. A young blonde woman came tentatively into the room and when she saw me she stopped. "I'm interrupting your visit," she said softly. "The nurse didn't say you had a guest."

Tyler motioned for her to come in. "Cailynn, this is Jane. Jane, this is Cailynn."

I stood to shake her hand and could see she was trembling. I had a feeling she already knew who I was. "Cailynn, it's nice to meet you," I said smiling.

She took my hand but her eyes didn't meet mine. "I'm glad to finally meet you," she said blushing.

I stood there for a moment feeling extremely uncomfortable. "Um, so Cailynn, I was just leaving. You can stay and keep Tyler company. My fiancé is probably wondering where I am." At the word fiancé, Cailynn's eyes met mine. I saw the confusion in her eyes and I had to fix this. "I was just telling Tyler about my engagement and he was telling me about you."

She seemed relieved. "Congratulations. I hope you'll be very happy." I waved goodbye to Tyler and walked to the door.

I was behind the curtain out of their view when I heard Tyler say, "Cailynn, why are you here? How did you find me?"

"I thought you were dead. I heard from Mark that you'd been in a horrible accident. I've been praying for you to wake up so I could have the chance to tell you how I feel. I love you Tyler. I've loved you from the first day I met you but didn't have the courage to tell you. Then one day you just disappeared and I knew you'd come back here to Jane. I need to know how you feel. Are you in love with her or are you willing to try again with me?"

I felt so guilty eavesdropping but I couldn't help but listen. I heard him say, "I thought I wanted Jane and the life we used to have but now I realize that was just a delusion. I need to start my life over and if you're willing, I'd like to try to start over with you. I really do care about you, I just don't have much to offer except my promise to try to do better."

I heard her sob and the creak of the bed as they embraced. Smiling, I turned the knob and left the room. I reached the waiting room and saw Jay pacing back and forth. He looked up as I came in and our eyes met. I raced into his arms and he wrapped his arms tightly around me. "I'm so glad you're here," I whispered.

"I wouldn't be anywhere else," he said softly. "I love you, babe."

"I love you, too," I said before giving him a gentle kiss. "I think we're all going to be okay. Tyler has decided to give up his rights to Jolene and I do believe he's going to be just fine. This accident has been the wake-up call he needed to try to get his life back on track. He also knows we're engaged and that I love you and only you." I squeezed him tightly and snuggled into his chest.

Jay sighed, "I hope this is the end of all the drama for your sake. I'll be completely convinced once it's official."

Looking up at him, I nodded, "I'm going to have the lawyer get the necessary paperwork and have him sign right away. I don't want him to get a chance to change his mind."

We walked out of the hospital holding hands and it was then I realized I hadn't even asked about Jolene. As if reading my mind, Jay smiled. "Our little one is safe with Callie and Justin. I'm thankful they knew where you were."

Jay got me tucked in my car and followed me over to Callie and Justin's. Jolene was sitting in the hallway playing with Mrs. Callahan's poodle that seemed to be the most active I'd ever seen him. As soon as she saw us, she jumped up and ran to throw herself in my arms. "Mama! Daddy! Can I have a puppy? I love this puppy, he's nice and gives me kisses. Can I, pleeeeease?"

Jay started laughing at her breathless barrage. "Sweet Pea, puppies are a lot of work. Mrs. Callahan has all day to take care of hers. You have to go to school and what's he going to do all day when you're there?"

She poked out her bottom lip and I saw it begin to quiver. She was pulling out the big guns. "But, Daddy." The quivering intensified. I could see Jay going through a mental struggle between common sense and wanting to please her. I kept out of it because, truth be told, I wouldn't mind a little dog to grow up with Jolene but we'd always lived in an apartment and weren't able to have one. Jay looked at me for back up and I gave him a sappy grin.

He finally threw up his hands. "I'll think about it. I'm not saying yes but I'm also not saying no."

Jolene squealed and the poodle barked with excitement. "When I get home I'm gonna draw you a picture of my puppy."

Under his breath, Jay said to me, "Maybe she'll forget by the time we get home."

"Don't count on it," I said giggling. "She has a mind like a steel trap. She won't forget." After saying goodnight to Callie and Justin, we headed back home and just like she'd promised, Jay got twelve drawings of "her" puppy.

****

Jay

Jane and I talked about the dog situation after Jolene went to bed. I'd admitted that I'd always been too busy to have a pet but had always imagined myself with a yellow Lab sitting faithfully beside my wingback chair in front of a roaring fire. Unfortunately, the pictures Jolene drew were of a tiny wire-haired spotted dog and I didn't think I would be able to convince her that a Lab would be a better choice. I also didn't want a dog that would outweigh her by the time it was six months old, so we decided the best action was to go to the animal shelter and find a young dog that would fit her puppy description as closely as possible. I got up the next morning and found Jolene busy scribbling another picture of her puppy and decided to let her know what we'd decided.

"Sweet Pea, I love the pictures you've been drawing and I want you to keep all of them together because as soon as we can, we're going to go looking for him." She looked up at me with those eyes and saw them suddenly brimming with tears. "Hey, what's wrong? Why're you crying?" I said kneeling down in front of her tea party table where she had all of her crayons scattered around.

"Daddy, you're really gonna get me a puppy?" Her bottom lip was quivering and I could tell she was just seconds from bawling. I quickly wiped her eye with my thumb and thought fast.

"Only if you'll stop crying. Puppies only want to come home with happy little girls," I said scooping her up into a hug. She buried her face in my shoulder and I could feel her fighting back the tears.

"Th—thank you," she sniffled. "I promise I'll take care of him." I nodded and held her close. I looked up to see Jane standing at the door. She was smiling and had an "I told you so" look on her face and I had to laugh.

"So, we're getting a puppy, huh?" She asked as she came up to us and, placing her hand on Jolene's back, began to rub in gentle circles.

Jolene raised her head from my shoulder. "Yeah, and he's gonna be my very own."

I looked at that now smiling face and realized how much it meant to me to make her and Jane happy. They were my world and I'd do anything to have those smiles on their faces every day.

Jane and I took all of Jolene's pictures and put them into a folder which we marked 'Puppy' and put it beside the front door so we would be sure to remember it when we went on our puppy hunt. We dropped Jolene off at daycare and heard Miss Torri being updated on the exciting news. I had a feeling she was going to end up with some pictures of 'Puppy' too.

Jane and I went straight to the attorney's office. I dropped her off so she could get information about how to get the termination of parental rights paperwork started. I ran to the office and got started opening mail and returning phone calls. Callie and Justin came in together and I knew I'd be seeing more of him as the time got closer for the baby to arrive. Callie insisted on working until she popped and as I watched her waddle over to the copier, I figured it wouldn't be too much longer. Justin tried to do it for her but she smacked his hands away and told him to chill out. I had to laugh.

Poor guy was turned upside down over this baby and I really couldn't blame him.

Jane arrived about an hour later and she had some legal documents that the attorney had prepared for Tyler to sign. She walked into my office and tossed them on the desk.

"We need him to sign these, with witnesses and return them to the court for processing then the court will determine from these papers if his rights will be terminated," she said perching on the side of my desk. I couldn't resist running my hand up her bare leg and she glanced around to see if anyone was watching before she gave me a big smile. "Um, is someone feeling frisky this morning?" She said waggling her brows at me.

"Maybe. Is someone interested in a quick trip home for lunch?" I said returning the waggle.

"Babe, I'd love to but I was going to run these to the hospital and get Tyler to sign them. Do you want to go with me?" I was still caressing her leg and she put her hand on mine. "I really would like for you to come."

"Hmm, hot lunch sex or getting papers signed. What to do, what to do?" I appeared to be in deep thought.

"Funny guy, you know the papers need to be done. The hot sex can happen anytime, anywhere. You've got me now, Mister. You liked it and you put a ring on it."

I laughed out loud. "Oh is that how that works? I should have put a ring on it a little sooner then. I've got some catching up to do." I scooted my chair back and stood getting ready to give her a little taste of what lunch could have been like when Justin knocked at the door.

"Hey guys, am I interrupting?" He said laughing at my obvious disappointment at being most definitely interrupted. "Um, Callie's got a doctor's appointment this afternoon and I'll be going with her. The doctor's going to let us know how much further they think she can go."

Jane popped up off the desk. "Oh Justin, this is so exciting! I know you can't wait. I know she's got to be getting really close. Are they watching the size of the baby in case his being big could cause complications?"

"Yeah, she has what the doctor called "a narrow pelvis" and it may not be possible for her to deliver naturally if the baby is too big. We'll find out today, I guess."

Jane was all excited. "You'll have to call me and let me know. I was trying to plan a shower before the baby gets here but with all the stuff with Tyler, it's gotten away from me."

Justin smiled, "Jane, we've got everything under control and you can throw her a shower after the baby comes. It'll be just fine."

Callie walked in behind Justin and said, "What'll be just fine?" He turned and pulled her to him placing his hand protectively over her tummy.

"Jane throwing you a shower after the baby gets here. You don't mind, do you? We've already done the nursery so it's not like you need things to get that done."

"You did the nursery?" Jane exclaimed. "Where was I? I was supposed to help you decorate!"

Callie smiled and put her hand on Jane's arm to calm her. "Justin surprised me by doing the whole room while I was napping the other day. It turned out beautifully and it's all ready for little Ryder to come home."

Jane relaxed and smiled. "Okay, I'll forgive you this time but the next kid you guys have, I want to help out more."

Justin had to say what we were all thinking, "Jane, you can help AFTER conception."

She looked at him dumbfounded for a moment then rolled her eyes and started laughing. "Yes, I'll definitely wait until after the conception to help you, dork."

Callie and Justin headed out to go to the doctor and I grabbed my keys to lock up the office so we could head to the hospital.

When we arrived, we were informed that Tyler had been moved to a regular room and that he could have visitors. Jane led me to his room but I balked at the door. "I don't want him getting pissed at me and not signing the papers," I said stubbornly.

Jane rolled her eyes but went in by herself and was only gone a few minutes when she came back to the door. "He wants to talk to you, alone," she said taking me by the hand.

Reluctantly, I let her lead me into the room. I saw Tyler sitting up in bed, the bedside tray was in front of him and the papers we'd brought were sitting there unsigned. Jane looked at me and smiled. "Since you've never been formally introduced, Tyler this is Jay." Tyler reached out his hand and I shook it. Jane excused herself and left us alone except for the nurse who had agreed to be a witness.

"Have a seat, Jay," Tyler said indicating the chair next to the bed. I walked over and sat, anxiously waiting to hear what he could possibly need to talk to me about. "So, Jane brought me these papers and I'm fully prepared to sign them but I need to talk to you, man to man, first."

I leaned back in the chair watching him closely. "What do you want to talk about?" I finally said.

"Jane has told me that you are in love and plan to get married. She also tells me that Jolene sees you as her daddy. I guess I can see now that biology has nothing to do with being a dad. I obviously suck at it."

I shrugged my shoulders. "Tyler, you were messed up when you ran away. There's no excuse for leaving Jane pregnant, but I can see you couldn't possibly have been thinking straight."

"Yeah, well, the only thing I need to know from you is that you will take care of my little girl like she was your own. I want you to promise me that you'll never let her down like I did. I have to tell you…having a near-death accident can sure make you reassess your life and all I've seen so far is failure and disappointment. I want Jolene to have the best dad in the world and I know now that it's not me."

I shifted in my chair. I actually was feeling sorry for the poor guy. "Look Tyler, I know you are a young guy with a long life ahead of you. You need to get your life straight before you can think of sharing that life with someone. One step at a time is the way to go."

He nodded. "Yeah, I guess I had deluded myself that my future still included Jane and Jolene, but she's told me how much she loves you and I think it's time to finally let go." He picked up the pen, checked the boxes on the form and signed at the bottom by the red 'Sign Here' arrow. I saw a tear roll down his cheek as he laid the pen down and I took a deep breath with relief but also with sadness. Tyler's pain was my gain and it felt bittersweet.

"Jay, could you do me a favor?" He asked. "Could you ask Jane to come in for a moment?" I nodded and left to get Jane.

I saw a young lady who had been sitting next to Jane. We sat in silence for a few moments then she softly spoke, "I'm Cailynn. You must be Jay." I nodded and she continued, "Tyler's not really a bad person. He's just messed up from a lot of bad things that have happened to him. I'm not making excuses because there really aren't any for what he did but he's willing to try to do better and I'm going to help him. I really love him and hope that one day he'll feel the same way about me."

I looked at her and smiled, "He'd be a fool not to."

Jane came out of the room a moment later holding the paper in one hand and wiping tears with the other. "Cailynn, he wants you to go in now," she said as she came closer. Cailynn stood and we watched as she quietly excused herself to head back to his room.

Jane waited until we heard the door close and then she grabbed me and held me tightly. I wrapped my arms around her and buried my face in her neck. We stood silently for several minutes, both of us realizing this was the ending of one thing but the beginning of another. We finally pulled back and looked into each other's eyes.

"It's over," she whispered. I nodded and gently leaned in to touch my forehead to hers.

Chapter 6

Callie

Justin and I arrived at Dr. Davidson's office a few minutes early so I found a seat near the television and saw they had a soap opera on. It was one I hadn't seen in years but the characters were still the same, albeit older. Within a few minutes, I was engrossed in the story as if I'd been following it for years. I was staring at the screen watching the evil tycoon lording over his poor long-suffering wife. Her lover, the totally hot pool boy, was hiding behind the big palm tree waiting to soothe her the moment he left. I heard the secretary call someone back for their appointment and I just kept watching until I felt Justin's eyes boring into me.

"What?" I finally said looking at him while rolling my eyes.

"They called your name, Callie," he said shaking his head with disbelief.

"Oh," I laughed. "Sorry." I hefted my rotund self out of the chair and that's when it happened. I heard a soft pop and then felt a huge gush and looked down to see that my water had broken all over my chair and the floor.

Justin's eyes practically bugged out of his head. "Is that supposed to happen?" He said with his voice about two octaves higher than normal. I was about to respond when the nurse and my doctor came running into the waiting room pushing a wheelchair. They gently guided me into it and pushed me back into the exam room. Dr. Davidson helped me onto the table and did a quick exam. "Well, Callie, you've really started labor this time but nothing urgent. We'll have time to get you to the hospital before this little guy gets here."

Justin stood quietly by watching and I knew he was a millisecond away from freaking out so I calmly told him to call our family and friends and let them know we were going to be headed to the hospital. He leapt into action calling my mom, his dad and then Jay and Jane. I could hear the concern in Jane's voice as she asked if I was okay. Justin asked her to run by our place and pick up my baby bag. Surprisingly, I was very calm. Almost too calm in fact. I was waiting for the nerves to kick in and my heart to start racing but it was almost as if I was watching everything happen from outside myself. Dr. Davidson had an ambulance come to the office to take me to the hospital and Justin followed behind in the car. It was a short ride and within minutes I was being unloaded and taken up to the fourth floor Labor and

Delivery. They got me admitted and rolled me down to one of the LDR rooms. It looked like a hotel suite and I felt very comfortable. They got me undressed and put me into a gown and got me situated in the bed to await Dr. Davidson's assessment of what was next. I hadn't had any pains yet so I really wasn't sure this was it but the nurse assured me that once my water broke there was no going back.

Justin was pacing back and forth in front of my bed and I was getting ready to see if I could toss a water pitcher that far when I heard her. My mom. She was walking down the hallway talking to everyone she saw.

"My baby's having a baby. I'm so excited. Yes, she's having a boy. I'm here to help her. It's her first. She has a narrow pelvis." She didn't stop until she got to my room.

"Really, Mom? Do you have to tell everyone the condition of my pelvis?" I asked as she breezed in. She just ignored me and walked over to hug Justin. "Hello? Mom? Aren't you here for me?" I asked with my lip poked out.

"Oh Callie, you're a big girl. Justin is scared out of his mind right now. He needs a hug." She was still fussing over Justin when Dr. Davidson walked in.

"Okay, everybody but dad out right now. I need to do an exam," he said looking specifically at my mom.

Not intimidated in the least, she walked right over and stood next to him. He looked her up and down and said, "Ma'am, I'd really like to do this exam with just my patient and her husband."

I saw my mom bristle and really wanted to warn him but figured I'd just let him find out on his own. "Look, I gave birth to that child myself. I have seen every inch of her body so there's nothing new to see here. If she wants me to leave, then I'll leave but otherwise, I'm here for the delivery."

Dr. Davidson looked at me and I could only shrug. "It's fine if she stays. It'll probably be easier on all of us if she does," I said rolling my eyes.

He nodded and began my exam. Watching everything he was doing, Justin paled considerably and sat over in the corner. After checking me thoroughly, Dr. Davidson snapped off his rubber glove and basically told me I was in for a long night. He gave me some meds to make me comfortable and said he would just have to watch me through the night for signs of labor. I was barely feeling any contractions, no worse than the Braxton Hicks so I was pretty comfortable. The only discomfort I was feeling was from the constant pillow-fluffing, bed moving, and television channel changing my mother was doing as she clucked around my bed.

I sat there thinking back to our discussion of our birth plan with my doctor and for some crazy reason (probably hormones) I had said I wanted my mom in there with Justin and I. What had I been thinking? I watched Justin lying on the couch with a piece of newspaper tented over his face and knew he was using it to hide his delight in my torment. He'd tried to talk me out of it, insisting that it would be more special with just the two of us but I'd dismissed it. Surely my mom would be somewhat respectful of me and my privacy and just sit quietly by while I labored along bringing her first grandchild into the world. No such luck. Every nurse who walked in got an in-depth description of my narrow pelvis, my fear of needles from childhood, and my low pain tolerance from the time I fell roller-skating and took off the top layer of my knee. In my defense, it frickin' hurt and I was only seven years old. I finally asked if I could get up and walk around so she wouldn't fluff me anymore. The nurse got me a robe and I grabbed my IV pole and my husband and left the room. My mom tried to follow but I told her that it was going to be a long night. I suggested she should run to get something to eat. Reluctantly, she grabbed her bag, kissed my cheek and told me not to have the baby until she got back. Like that was an option on my part. I could only shake my head.

Justin walked while I waddled and we made a few circuits around the L&D floor but then it hit me. The first contraction was like someone stuck a knife in my stomach and I had to stop and lean on the wall until it passed. The last five hundred feet to my room were like a mile and Justin was literally pushing me toward the room. He kept saying, "Don't you give birth to my son in the hallway!" I wanted to remind him that it was 'our' son but didn't have the breath once another contraction hit. The nurse saw our dilemma and helped me back to the room and into the bed. She then hooked me up to monitors and told me that my walking was probably done for the night. I felt like a trapped animal as soon as my mom came back in the room. Justin's dad Joe and his mom Dianne showed up so he left to give them a progress report. My mom sat in the chair by my bed watching me for any signs of discomfort and when she'd see me start to fidget, she'd leap into action, wiping my brow or rubbing my arm, basically anything she could do to irritate me. In the meantime, Dr. Davidson came in and checked me again and said I was progressing along nicely. Nicely? How in the hell did nicely describe what it felt like every time a contraction hit. They were coming closer together now and my patience was getting thinner. My mom offered me ice chips, but I wasn't in the mood. She looked disappointed that I wasn't jumping all over the wonderful things she was doing for me, but I really just wanted to be left alone.

"Callie, you really should keep hydrated with some ice chips. You're going to be panting pretty hard and all your membranes will be dry," she said pushing the ice chips back in front of me. I felt my irritation level hit maximum overload and I grabbed the cup and threw it at the door. Unfortunately, Justin was coming in at that moment and he got whacked right across the bridge of the nose with the cup and ice flew all over the room. He looked at me, his eyes wide and he slowly backed out of the room.

I heard a voice that sounded a bit possessed say, "Where's my epidural?" and I realized it was me. The nurse said I'd have to be dilated a certain amount before they would do it but she'd see what she could do. Between gritted teeth, I asked her if that wouldn't be too much trouble. My mom looked at me and started to say something but stopped when she saw my face. I heard the door open and saw the anesthesiologist bringing his magic cart of relief through the door. Within moments he had prepped me and inserted the epidural and brought me sweet blessed relief.

****

Justin

I was afraid to go back in. I'd been outside talking to my dad and mom when I figured I'd better make sure Callie hadn't killed her mom. I'd opened the door and had an ice cup hit me right across the bridge of my nose and I felt a shower of ice chips rain down inside my shirt as well as all over the floor. I backed out and turned to see my parents looking at me with expressions of sympathy and understanding. My dad clapped me on the shoulder and smiled. "Son, this is where it gets good. She's getting close."

My mom put her arm around me and gave me a squeeze. "I was in labor for a lot longer before I started throwing things. This is a good sign."

I stood staring at the door and felt a wave of panic come over me. "I'll be right back," I said turning and hauling ass down the hallway. I got to the elevators and hit both of the arrow buttons. I didn't know if I was going up or down, I just wanted out for a few minutes. The doors opened and I threw myself in and hit a button for a floor. When the doors opened, I realized I was on the children's floor. I saw little ones in wheelchairs and some walking with their moms and dads with IV poles attached to their little arms. A nurse came up to me and asked if I was looking for someone in particular. I stood there for a moment and then finally confessed I was escaping from the labor floor. She laughed and said she'd had four children of her own and her husband had escaped every time. I felt really stupid by this time and figured I'd better head back up to save Callie from her mom.

As the elevator doors opened, I saw my parents standing with Jay and Jane and they all had big smiles on their faces as I walked by with my head held high. I walked up to the door, took a deep breath and turned the handle. What I saw when I opened the door was nothing short of a miracle. My wife was holding hands with her mom and she had the most peaceful look on her face. Her mom was grinning from ear to ear. I almost didn't believe my eyes. I walked in and made eye-contact with the nurse. I raised my brows in question and as she walked by she whispered, "Epidural." Ah, that explained everything. I'd heard of this phenomenon and now I was seeing it live and in action.

"I love my mom!" Callie said beaming at her mother. Her mom was wearing a matching smile and I couldn't help but laugh. They both looked at me puzzled for a moment then Callie said, "I love you too, pookie." I really didn't want her mom to know she called me pookie but apparently we were in a love fest right now.

"I love you too, babe," I said walking over to stand beside her bed. "Can we keep the pookie to ourselves though?" I whispered as I kissed her cheek.

"Oh, pookie!" She said grinning, "Mom knows all about it so it's ok."

I forced a grin and threw myself in the chair by the bed. "Great!" I said rolling my eyes.

Callie's mom smiled sweetly but gave me a wink and excused herself for a moment. I sat next to Callie and absently rubbed her hand. She seemed so relaxed that I couldn't picture that a few minutes ago she'd been ready to snap my head off.

Dr. Davidson came in to do his check-up and I immediately saw a change in his attitude. "Well, Callie, you're completely dilated and ready to get this baby out!"

I felt the nurse tap me on the shoulder and say, "It's time." Things seemed to go into slow motion. Callie's mom came back into the room and stationed herself on one side of the bed and the nurse positioned me on the other. Callie seemed so calm and I wondered if it was because she knew this ordeal was almost over.

Dr. Davidson positioned Callie's legs in the stirrups and gave us instructions on how to best help her. I was to hold her hand and support her as she'd go into her push. I was happy to hold her hand because I actually didn't want that hand free to swing around and find the side of my face. I leaned in and kissed her forehead and she gave me a weak smile. "This is it, babe," I said softly. She nodded and then focused her attention on the doctor and his instructions. He would tell her to push and she'd grunt and groan and I'd find myself holding my breath with her. The frequency of the contractions became almost back to back and I was worried for her because it just seemed so exhausting. She was a trooper though, she never once screamed although I came close at one point when she put a particularly tight clench on my hand. I could feel the bones compressing and was just seeing spots before my eyes when the contraction eased and she in turn eased off the pressure. I heard the doc mention the word crowning and I flashed on the film we saw in the childbirth classes. He asked if I wanted to come and see and truthfully, I didn't. I preferred the bone-crushing grip of my beautiful wife and wanted to leave the image of her lady parts being pulled every which way but loose out of my mind. I looked up and saw Leslie leaning over to see what I had passed on and she smiled and squealed, "Oh, he's got a full head of hair!"

I was so tempted to look to see my son's entrance into the world but I also didn't want to. I squeezed my eyes shut and concentrated on supporting Callie as she pushed until I heard the doctor say, "He's here!"

I peeped my eyes open to see the most beautiful baby I'd ever seen in my life. The doctor placed him on Callie's stomach as they prepared the cord to be cut. I couldn't take my eyes off of him and I noticed my vision blurred as the tears came. I kissed Callie all over her face and told her I loved her with every kiss. She looked up at me and gave me a weak smile and I knew she was just as overwhelmed as I was. Dr. Davidson asked me if I'd like to cut the cord and I realized this was my job as dad. I needed to make that symbolic gesture so I took the funny scissors he gave me and cut the tough membrane holding them together. As soon as I finished, they whisked him away to the warming table and were wiping him off. I didn't want him to leave my sight but I also didn't want to leave Callie's side. She looked so exhausted but elated as well. I could see Ryder across the room and everyone was nodding and smiling so I assumed everything was good. Callie looked up at me and smiled. "Go see him, babe. Make sure he's okay." She didn't have to tell me twice! I made my way over to the table making sure I didn't get in their way. I heard them mention an APGAR score of 8 and 9 and a weight of 8lb. 6 oz. The nurse looked at me and said that he was perfect. I had to agree. He had pinked up now and they were dressing him in a little blue toboggan and a diaper. I saw all ten fingers and toes. Within a few moments, they had put a goopy substance in his eyes, had him wrapped up like a burrito and were trying to hand him to me. I stood there frozen for a moment. I was afraid that I'd be too clumsy to hold him correctly. The nurse saw my hesitation and smiled.

"He won't break. You can do this," she said handing him to me.

I put out my arms and felt his weight settle in. He looked up at me with his bleary eyes and I felt my heart melt. My eyes filled up with tears and I didn't care. I looked up and my eyes met Callie's. She was smiling but I could see tears rolling down her cheeks. The nurse snapped a special bracelet on my wrist that matched Callie and Ryder's and I walked carefully over to the bed and held him out to my beaming wife. She shook her head at first and I was confused. Finally, she was able to speak, "I love watching you with our baby. I want to remember this moment forever."

I swallowed back the lump that rose in my throat. I looked down again at the miracle that we had made together. It was the greatest feeling in the world. A few minutes later, Callie put her hands out and I settled Ryder against Callie's chest. He squirmed a little and made a tiny mewing noise but soon locked eyes with her and I watched in wonder as she put her finger in his palm and he wrapped his tiny fingers tightly around it. We sat like that for quite a while and Leslie took pictures of us. Finally, the nurse told us she needed to take him to the nursery for his shots and first bath. I must have looked anxious because she assured me he wouldn't be gone long and that if I wanted to watch, I could stand at the nursery window. I'd forgotten that I needed to tell everyone he was here so I told Callie that I'd go let the waiting room know he had safely arrived. I followed the nurse to the nursery and made sure he was safely inside before heading to the waiting room. As I walked in everyone came to their feet and smiling, I said, "He's here and he's perfect!" Everyone surrounded me with hugs and slaps on the back. My mom had tears streaming down her face and my dad had a grin from ear to ear. Tony had bubble gum cigars that he was handing out to the other people obviously waiting for news of their new arrival. Jane had the biggest smile of them all.

"Is Callie okay?" She asked touching my shoulder.

"Yeah, she's great. They're doing a little cleanup on her now and as soon as they move her to a room, I'll come get you and you can see her."

Leslie came out a few minutes later and she showed everyone the pictures on her camera. There were cries of "HE'S HUGE!" and "HE'S GORGEOUS!" I loved watching the family get their first look at my son.

Jane pulled me aside. She said to me seriously, "Are you okay? That didn't freak you out too badly, did it?"

I laughed, "No, I didn't look. I figured that was the best way to handle that."

Laughing with me she said, "I think you did the right thing."

About an hour later, the nurse came out to tell me that Callie had been moved into a room and that she could have visitors. I wanted the grandparents to see her first so I took them all back with me. Callie looked beautiful and grateful that she'd had a little time to freshen up. She got her congratulations from them all and posed for pictures. They were just getting ready to leave to let someone else visit when the nurse brought Ryder back in. I looked at Callie and she nodded. I picked Ryder up out of his bassinet and walked over to stand by the grandparents. "Everyone, I'd like to introduce you to Ryder Allen Brisson."

My dad's mouth fell open as did Leslie's. Allen was Callie's late father's name and it was also the middle name I shared with my dad. It was a name that covered everyone. Jolene gave us Ryder but Allen was going to be the tie to the family. Leslie burst into tears. "I had no idea," she sobbed. "What a beautiful tribute. I know he's here watching over us today." Tony put his arm around her and gave her a big hug.

My dad was still staring at me in disbelief. "You always hated your middle name," he said shaking his head. "I'm so honored but shocked."

"Dad, I never hated it. I was young and didn't realize what an honor it was to have your name in my own. Now, I know it's the right thing to do and Ryder will be blessed to have such a fine name." I looked down at my little man nestled in my arms and silently prayed for God's guidance in being the best dad I could be.

Chapter 7

Jane

After visiting Callie, Justin, and Ryder, we decided we'd better get into the office to get our work caught up. Jay and I were basically running everything and we still had some very important projects in the works. Mr. Davenport's bank building was coming along nicely and it was bringing a lot of attention to the firm. Jay was constantly returning phone calls about new projects and I was trying to schedule meetings for him and help with whatever preparation he needed. We made a great team and I realized this was what true happiness was.

I was sitting at my desk opening the mail when the phone rang. I answered and heard a voice I hadn't heard in a long time.

"Jane?"

I was too stunned to speak for a few moments. It was my mom.

"Jane?" She said again.

Finally I found my breath and managed to speak. "Hi," I said softly.

"It's been a long time," she began.

I couldn't help it. The tears started to flow down my cheeks. I had resigned myself to never hearing her voice again and here she was talking to me out of the blue.

"Yes," I managed to say.

"I'm calling because we heard about Tyler's accident and wondered how you were holding up," she said with concern.

I hesitated. How had they heard about the accident? "Well, he's doing okay now. His girlfriend called me this morning and told me that he's going to be released from the hospital within a few days and then I think he's heading back to Portland."

"Girlfriend? What do you mean? Aren't you two together?" She sounded confused.

"No!" I scoffed. "We haven't been together for the last five years. He left right after I told him I was pregnant," I said angrily.

There was silence then she spoke, "Pregnant? Do you have a child?"

I realized right then that I'd said too much but I couldn't take it back. "Yes. I have a daughter, Jolene." I heard the phone muffle as if someone was covering it. After a moment I said, "Are you still there?" I listened closely.

I heard a sniffle and then she spoke, "Yes, oh God Jane. We let pride get in the way of calling you and now we have a grandchild we don't even know. We've been so foolish."

I sat there stunned. I didn't know what to say. A few moments passed and finally my mom said what I thought I'd never hear, "I'm sorry."

I took a deep breath and all the tears I'd been holding back, all the pain and heartbreak I'd kept locked in my heart came pouring out with just those two words. I heard her breakdown and we sat and cried together for all the time lost. I heard my dad's voice in the background and I felt chills hearing it for the first time in years as well. I heard him take the phone from her and he spoke, "You there, Janie?" I managed to sob out a yes. "Just listen, okay? I've been a stubborn old fool and I can't even begin to count the times I've picked up the phone to call you but the thought of you choosing Tyler over us always stopped me. When we heard Tyler had been in an accident, your mom finally convinced me that we needed to see if you needed anything and now I hear that you haven't even been with him all this time…I just don't know what else to say except I'm sorry."

I took a deep breath and said, "I've missed you guys." I was now crying but laughing at the same time. I felt a hand on my shoulder and looked up to see Jay standing beside me.

"You okay, babe?" He whispered.

I nodded and mouthed 'my parents' as I pointed at the phone. A smile spread across his face and he nodded. He hugged me and left me to talk to them.

We talked for a while and I caught them up on my life. They were thrilled to find out I was engaged and I told them all about Jay and how wonderful he was to Jolene.

"So, when's the big day?" My dad asked.

"Umm, we haven't set a date yet. We've had some things going on that we needed to get cleared up. I'm not really sure."

"Well, when you figure it out, we'll be there," he said firmly. I heard my mom squeal in the background. "I know I've not been the best dad but I would be honored to give you away."

I was speechless for a moment then found my voice, "I'd like that." I couldn't contain the tears. "Well, you keep us informed, Janie. I can't wait to see you and meet that little granddaughter of mine. Here's your mom, she's practically climbing my back to get the phone."

My mom got back on and we talked about how tall Jolene was and she asked if they could Skype with her. I knew she was excited but I also had to figure out a way to explain a brand new set of grandparents to Jolene. "Let me get back with you on that, Mom," I finally said.

"I understand. She has no idea we exist, does she?" She said sounding a bit hurt.

"Mom, you have to understand. I wasn't going to make up stories about you and Dad. I just didn't say anything at all. Give me time to get her comfortable with the idea and maybe we can Skype together then."

She breathed deeply. "I know you're right but I'm so excited to see what she looks like. Can you text me a picture, at least?"

"Yeah, I can do that. Let me find a recent one and I'll send it." I scrolled through my phone and found a picture of Jolene I'd snapped while she was sleeping the other morning. "Mom, I'm sending one now." I hit the send button and heard a beep as the message went through. Within seconds I heard a squeal.

"Oh my God! She's beautiful! Look at that hair! What color eyes does she have?"

"Blue, like mine," I said smiling smugly to myself.

"Jane, she's beautiful. I can't wait to meet her."

"Give me some time, Mom. We can't go from zero to sixty in one second. I have to prepare Jolene for all this."

I heard a huge sigh. "Thank you for at least being open to the idea," she said. "We'll call you again soon."

"Okay, you both take care." I said softly. "Thank you for calling."

I hung up the phone and felt the biggest grin come over my face. I looked up and saw Jay watching me from his office. I got up and walked in and perched on the edge of his desk. He scooted over in front of me resting his hands on my thighs. "So, tell me everything."

****

Jay

I looked up at the glowing face of my beautiful Jane and heard the excitement in her voice as she told me about her parents reaching out to her after all this time. When she told me that they mentioned coming to our wedding I took the opportunity and ran with it.

"So when is this wedding going to take place?" I said grinning.

She seemed embarrassed. "Well, Jay…I didn't want to rush you or anything. I would marry you today but I really have been waiting to talk with you about it."

"Well today wouldn't really give your family time to get here but let's make a date now. If I had my way, I'd throw you over my shoulder and take you to the courthouse right now but honestly, I only want you to have one wedding and it has to be perfect." I said gazing into those beautiful eyes that now were brimming with tears.

"Jay, I don't need a big wedding! I would be more than happy with a simple ceremony," she said blushing.

I stood up and wrapped my arms around her. "I want the big wedding so I can stand at the front of a church and watch the woman of my dreams walk down the aisle and the world will know I'm the luckiest man alive."

She snuggled into my chest and stroked my tie absently. "I guess I could do that for you, then," she said grinning.

"Well, let's see. How long do ladies need to plan the wedding of their dreams?" I said laughing.

Jane looked up and smiled. "The hardest part of planning a wedding is finding the perfect groom. I've already got that. I figure to get everything I need done…maybe a month?"

"So, let's say the third Saturday in September. I'll let my mom know and you can call your parents and give them a date now," I said with a grin.

"Oh Jay, I'm so happy. I really never thought I'd have the chance to get them back into my life. I'm so lucky to have you and Jolene and that would have been enough but to have my family accept me again really means a lot to me." She sighed and snuggled even tighter to me. "They want to Skype with her but I need to explain who they are first. Will you help me?"

I couldn't help but smile. "Of course I will. Jolene's super smart and will probably accept them like she's accepted everything else she's had thrown at her lately. I have a feeling she'll be just fine."

I heard the front door open and saw Tristan O'Neal walk in. I expected Jane to jump back since a client walked in but she leisurely backed out of my arms and gave me a quick kiss on the lips before greeting him.

"Well, look who popped in," she said smiling.

"Hey Jane! Good to see you again," he said flashing a brilliant smile. I have to admit, I felt a twinge of jealousy watching their interaction but my heart said 'she belongs to you, get over it'.

"So, what can we do for you today, Tristan?" I said walking out of my office to shake his hand.

"Well, I came by to let you know that I'm going to be leaving town in a couple of months. My dad is really sick and my mom needs me to come home," he said with a deep sigh.

"Have a seat, Tristan. I hate to hear that about your dad." Jane said walking him to the couch in my office. "Can I get you anything? Coffee?"

"No thanks." He sat down and we joined him. "My dad has heart problems and he's been in and out of the hospital for the past couple of months. My brother lives nearby but is more interested in partying than helping my mom with dad. I had no idea things had gotten so bad until my mom finally broke down and told me. Ian, my brother, was supposed to be helping take them to my dad's doctor appointments and keeping an eye on things but so far he's only got his eye on the girls at the beach."

"Where are you from, Tristan?" Jane asked.

"I grew up in Kure Beach and moved to the big city to go to UNC-Charlotte. My brother never aspired to further his education so he stayed around the beach and does lifeguarding and surf lessons." He shook his head.

"I thought he'd be more responsible but apparently not. He's always had a chip on his shoulder and when I confronted him about not helping our parents, he copped a major attitude and hasn't spoken to me or them since. I've got to go back home to straighten things out. I've got a job lined up at a bank down there but I'm going to miss being here. Mr. Davenport has been so good to me. He gave me a chance and really was a mentor. I'm going to be starting over at a new bank but the CEO knows Mr. Davenport and I came highly recommended."

"Well, I think you're awesome for helping your parents," Jane said smiling. "We'll miss working with you but who knows what new adventures you'll have. Plus, we'll know someone at the beach when we head out for vacations."

We all laughed. Tristan nodded. "Absolutely! I'll definitely hook you up with all the great things to do and see."

We went over some of the final details of the new bank building and after an hour, Tristan left. Jane got a call from Callie and found out they were going to be letting them go home from the hospital the next morning. Ryder was doing fantastic and Callie had gotten the all clear from her doctor. Jane couldn't wait to share the news of our upcoming wedding and from the squeal on the other end of the conversation, I could tell Callie was excited. Jane called her parents and gave them the update on the wedding date and promised to get in touch with them soon about the possibility of Skyping with Jolene.

Tired from a busy day, we picked up Jolene who was so excited to share the pictures she'd drawn of her puppy and I knew this was going to have to be a priority on our list of things to do. We decided the best place to keep her attention was in the car so we casually brought up the news of her grandparents.

Jane began speaking to me, "You know, Callie's mom is so happy to be a grandma now that Ryder's here."

I watched Jolene in the mirror as she looked at her mom. "Ms. Leslie's a grandma? How do you get to be a grandma?"

Jane turned back to look at her, "Well, Ms. Leslie is a grandma because she is Callie's mom and Ryder is Callie's son. Callie is Ryder's mom and Leslie is his grandma." She looked back at me and rolled her eyes. Under her breath she muttered, "That sounded intelligent."

"Give her a minute to sort this out. You're not giving her credit here," I whispered.

A few moments went by. "Daddy, is your mom going to be my grandma when we get married?" I smiled and nodded at Jane who now had her mouth hanging open.

"Yes, Sweet Pea. She's going to be your grandma." I had a smug grin. That's my girl, I thought.

"Mama, do you have a mom too?"

"Here she goes," I said grinning.

Jane poked me before answering. "Yes, baby. I have a mom and a dad but they live far away from here. They are your grandma and grandpa."

She seemed thoughtful for a moment. "Why don't they come see me?" I looked at Jane and saw her take a deep breath. She seemed to struggle with her words so I jumped in.

"Sweet Pea, they live so far away that they couldn't come visit but they would love to see you on the computer. They also want to come see you when your mom and I get married." I saw Jane relax against the seat and mouth 'thank you' to me.

"Can we Skype with them, Mama?" She asked while bouncing in her seat.

"Jolene, how do you know about Skype?" Jane asked with confusion.

"Ms. Maegan used to Skype with Mr. Nate when he was driving his truck far away. She used to tell us to be as quiet as a mouse when she was talking to him but she used to let us say hi."

Jane threw up her hands and laughed. "Of course she knows what Skype is, she's almost five!" She shook her head.

Jolene thought that was funny and burst out in a giggle fit. "Well, Mama? Can we?"

Jane reached back to take Jolene's hand. "Of course we can, sweetie. I'll call them and set it up."

"Yay! Maybe they'll eat dinner with me and watch Spongebob," she said smiling.

We drove the rest of the way home fielding questions about where they lived and how long until the wedding. Jane called her parents when she got in the house and since they were three hours behind us, we decided the best thing to do was to let Jolene get wound down from her day, take her bath and get in her pjs. At seven, we turned on the computer and Jane sat down to get it started in case Jolene got shy. I doubted very much that was going to be the case but we were prepared. I sat next to Jane with Jolene on my lap. Jane made the Skype call and within moments the connection was made. I saw a beautiful blonde woman who looked like an older version of Jane on the screen next to a man who at first glance reminded me of Chuck Norris. They were sitting at what appeared to be a kitchen table. They could only see Jane at first and I heard the surprise in their voices when they saw her.

"Jane, you look so different, so grown-up," her mom said.

"Well, I'm not a teenager anymore," she said laughing.

Her mom laughed too. "I guess not. You're a beautiful woman and a mother now. It's hard to believe how much we've missed." The talked for a few more minutes about family updates and I could tell they were anxiously awaiting the first glimpse of their granddaughter. Jane continued to speak with them and I could tell Jolene was curious but she didn't want them to see her just yet. She clung to my shoulder just out of view of the webcam.

Jane asked them about their day and they told her that they'd been out walking around downtown Portland looking at the fountain at Salmon Street. Jane grew up there and knew exactly where they'd been. They told her they had seen several children playing in the fountain. I saw Jolene perk up at the mention of the fountain since the Pack Square fountain was a favorite of hers. She slowly leaned over into the view of the webcam. They spotted her and both said, "Hey!" and it sent her retreating back out of their view. Cautiously, she leaned back in and this time they didn't scare her off. She waved and they waved. She grinned and they grinned. It was several minutes of pantomime until finally Jolene said, "Hi Grandma and Grandpa."

Their faces lit up and I could see them studying her features obviously looking for something familiar. Finally, Jane's mom spoke, "Jolene, you have the prettiest hair I've ever seen!"

Jolene patted her hair with her hand. "Thank you, Grandma. I don't like to get it brushed. It hurts my head."

Jane looked at Jolene with confusion. "It hurts to get your hair brushed? Why am I just finding this out?"

Jolene smiled. "I didn't want you to worry, Mama."

Jane laughed. "Well, I'm glad we're getting all of this out tonight."

Jolene giggled and wanted to show them her Rapunzel doll. They oohed and ahhed over it appropriately. She wanted to show them Spongebob but we reminded her that they wanted to talk to her and not watch tv. She seemed disappointed but she quickly rallied back with my introduction.

"Grandma, Grandpa…this is my daddy!" I leaned in to wave at the webcam and saw they were studying me now.

Jane's father spoke up, "Jay is it? I'm Paul and this is my wife Sharon. We're very pleased to meet you and are very happy to hear you're going to be marrying our Jane. What exactly do you do for a living, if I may ask?"

I knew this was coming but it didn't stop the sweaty palms. "I'm an architect. I'm a partner at the firm where Jane works."

Her dad's eyes grew bigger. "A partner! Did you hear that Sharon? That's pretty impressive for someone your age. How old are you, if you don't mind my asking?"

"I don't mind you asking. I'm thirty. I made partner when I was twenty-six at The Mathewson Group and have since moved on to form a partnership with Jane's former boss at the same group and we took Jane along with us." Jane put her hand on my arm and smiled.

"Oh my God. Look at that ring!" Her mom squealed. "That is the most beautiful ring I've ever seen in my life." Jane held her hand up to the camera to let her mom inspect it and I felt pretty good about their opinion of me versus Tyler at that point.

Her dad leaned back in his chair. "Son, I need to tell you something. Despite me acting like a stupid a-- oops, sorry a-s-s, I love my baby girl and always have. I hope you can make her happy like she deserves to be."

"Sir, I'm going to do my best to make her happy for the rest of her life and I'll make that promise before God and everyone on our wedding day." I squeezed Jolene and gave her a kiss on the cheek. "I also promise to be the best dad I can to Jolene. She's my little girl just as much as if she were my own flesh and blood." I looked at Jane and smiled. "I also plan to legally adopt her as soon as we're married so she can have my last name as well." Jane's eyes filled with tears. She leaned over and hugged me tightly and gave me a soft kiss on the cheek.

Paul cleared his throat with emotion. "I'm very happy to hear that. We're very excited about the wedding and visiting with you all."

Sharon leaned into the view of the webcam. "I'm going to start calling airlines tomorrow to see what the cheapest flight is and I'll go ahead and book it."

I had to speak up, "Mr. and Mrs. Carter...I'd like to take care of your tickets as a wedding gift to Jane. I'll make all the arrangements and book you into a hotel here and take care of everything."

Sharon leaned back and I saw her mouth fall open. "Are you sure? We have enough money to get there."

"I insist. I'll call the airline in the morning and make all the arrangements." I leaned over and kissed

Jane on the cheek. "The best gift I can give my girls for our wedding is their family."

Paul and Sharon both smiled and nodded. It was about that time that Jane and I noticed Jolene fading fast so we let her tell them goodnight and we wished them the same. They blew kisses at her and she blew kisses back and we closed out of the Skype session.

I carried my sleepy girl to her bedroom and Jane and I tucked her in. I kissed her on the forehead and watched her yawn. "Night, Daddy. Night, Mama. I'm glad I got Grandma and Grandpa for our wedding."

Jane gave her a kiss and we turned off the light. We stood at the door watching her slowly fall asleep, her arm wrapped tightly around Rapunzel.

I wrapped my arms around Jane and nuzzled her neck. "You've had a pretty emotional day. I think a bubble bath is in order."

I kissed her gently and took her by the hand. I led her to our bathroom and started the bath water running. I'd bought some bubble bath since I'd been lacking in that department before my girls moved in and I put a dab in the tub to get some suds going. She stood watching me with a smile on her face. "When did you become an expert at bubble baths, Mr. Anderson?"

"Well, I met this beautiful woman who has this equally beautiful little girl who wanted to take a bath in my tub and all I had was some body wash to make bubbles. I went right out the next day and bought some proper bubble bath to make my girls happy."

I put my hand under the stream of water to check the temperature and then turned back to Jane. I slowly started unbuttoning her blouse and found a lacy pink bra underneath. I leaned in and kissing the hollow of her neck, slid her blouse completely off. I then unbuttoned her skirt and slid it down her hips letting it pool around her ankles. My eyes lingered on her matching panties and long athletic legs. I turned her away from me and brushed her hair over her shoulder and kissed the nape of her neck. I could see tiny goose bumps rise on her skin and I knew I'd found her sweet spot. I unhooked her bra and slid it off tossing it to the side. I hooked my thumbs in her panties and slid them slowly down letting her lean on me to step out of them. The water in the tub was just right and she started to step in but stopped. "You're going to join me, Mr. Anderson," she purred.

She reached up and loosened my tie until she could slide it out of my collar. My tie joined her lacy garments on the floor and then she slowly started unbuttoning my shirt. My hands slid onto her hips and she gently smacked them away. "No, sir. No touching...yet." After undoing every button, she slid it off my shoulders and kissed the hollow of my neck. "Turnabout is fair play, Mr. Anderson." I had to admit, her calling me Mr. Anderson was really hot. She undid my belt and slid it out of my belt loops and then unbuttoned my pants. They dropped to the floor and I stepped out of them leaving only my boxers and my socks. She started to reach down to take them off but I quickly kicked out of the boxers and yanked my socks off. "In a hurry, are we?" She giggled.

She stepped into the tub and settled into the cloud of bubbles. I climbed in and sat behind her letting her lean back against me. I wrapped my arms around her and I felt her relax. She turned her head and her mouth found mine. We shared a long sweet kiss, one full of emotion, passion and promise. She turned to face me and took the washcloth, soaped it up and started gently washing my chest. She feathered kisses along my jaw and I slid my hands up her soapy skin. Our kisses became more passionate and I knew it was time to dry off and take this to the bedroom. I climbed from the tub and helped her climb out. She looked up at me through those beautiful lashes and I saw the flash of her tongue and she slowly licked her lips. My heart started hammering in my chest just like it did every time she looked at me that way. Her hair was damp from the bath and she had that sweet vanilla scent that drove me wild every time she walked by. I wrapped my arms around her, our naked bodies slippery against each other. She snaked her hands into my hair and pulled me in for a sizzling kiss. I couldn't stop the groan that came deep from my chest and I cracked my eyes open to see the hint of a smile on her mouth. She was definitely pushing all the right buttons with me and she knew it. I backed her out of the bathroom never letting our lips part and when we got to our bed, I spun her around and fell backwards pulling her on top of me. She purred and started biting my neck and I felt my eyes roll back in my head. Our mouths locked in a frenzied kiss and I ended up rolling her over onto her back. I broke the kiss and lifted myself over her to look into her eyes. "You know you drive me crazy, right?" I said watching her panting from our last kiss. She didn't reply, she just reached around and pulled me back down for another kiss until we were lost in the sensations and without words we made passionate love until we were left breathless. I laid my head against her chest as she ran her fingers through my hair and kissed my forehead. I was feeling so much love for her at that moment that I had to say what I was thinking. "Jane?" I whispered.

"Mmmm?" She softly sighed.

"I want to try to have a baby as soon as possible," I said looking up to see her reaction.

I saw tears well up in her eyes. "Jay, I'd love to have a baby with you. I have to be totally honest with you and tell you that it scares the hell out of me though."

I scooted up to lay face to face with her. "Why are you scared, babe?" I said as I tucked a piece of hair behind her ear.

"I know this is going to sound stupid," she said softly. "I'm afraid because the last time I got pregnant, I was left alone. I know you won't do that to me but there's a part of me that still feels that fear that I'd find out, want to tell you and you'd be gone." Her face was so serious and it broke my heart to see how deeply Tyler had hurt her.

"Jane, I'm not Tyler. I love you and want to marry you as soon as possible. I want to be Jolene's daddy and I want a child that's as beautiful as you and as charming as me." I gave her a goofy grin and I saw the hint of a smile. "I want to be there from the moment we conceive to the moment our child comes into this world. I don't want to miss a single moment of your cravings, your sonograms, the baby's first kick…I'm in this for good."

She placed her hands on both sides of my face and softly kissed me. "How did I get so lucky? Until we met, I thought men like you only existed in romance novels. Jay, God willing, we will have a child. I pray that child is just like his or her daddy."

I kissed her and pulled her body close to me again. We fell asleep wrapped in each other's arms.

Chapter 8

Callie

We came home from the hospital and put Ryder in his bassinet and realized we had a problem. He was so big that it tilted to the side. I looked at Justin and laughed. "We sure know how to make a healthy baby, that's for sure." I laid him on the bed until we could figure out what to do and watched in amazement as he tried to roll over. He was only three days old but seemed to be far more advanced than that. We realized that despite all our best planning, Ryder wasn't going to fit the bassinet so into the crib he went. Justin had left for a few minutes to grab some groceries so I was alone with my baby. Jane and Jay were bringing Jolene over to see him today because she had absolutely worried them to death about it. I was expecting them but I really didn't feel like dressing up for company, so I had on my huge Panthers t-shirt and some loose shorts. I felt so fat and stretched out of shape that I didn't want anyone to see me. Justin had tried to come into the bathroom when I was taking a shower right after we got home and I freaked out on him. He backed out and I know he was thinking it was hormones and part of it was. The other part was the insecurity I'd had all my life about my body. My feelings were multiplied times ten and I didn't know how to stop it. Right after I got home I tried to figure out how to exercise without Justin finding out. My doctor had specifically told me not to do any serious exercising until I'd been back for my checkup but all I could think about was fitting into the jeans I wore before I got pregnant.

I heard the buzzer for the door and jumped up to grab it before it woke Ryder who was napping. It was Jay and Jane, so I buzzed them in and glanced in the mirror. I saw a tired puffy face staring back at me and didn't like it one bit. I ran to the bathroom and tried to throw some makeup on my face but it just made me feel worse seeing the result. I looked worse. I heard a quiet knock at the door and went to open it. My best friend looked at me as I opened the door and her face fell. I should've known I couldn't hide anything from her. Jay walked in holding Jolene's hand and her head was swiveling around looking for a sign of the baby. "He's sleeping right now Jolene, but he should be ready for a bottle soon."

"Okay, Aunt Callie. I can wait," she whispered. She walked over and sat down on the couch and folded her hands in her lap.

I looked at Jane for an explanation and she whispered, "Jay and I had a talk about using our 'inside voice' when we were around the baby."

We had just sat down when I heard a tiny cry. Jolene perked up immediately but stayed right on the couch. I got up to get him, carried him into the kitchen and was just about to get his bottle out of the fridge when I saw Jane reaching for it.

"Okay, we're all alone, what's going on?" She said taking the bottle and beginning to warm it.

"Nothing, I'm just tired," I lied.

"You can't fool me, woman. What's going on in that head of yours?" She persisted.

"I'm sure it's nothing. I'm sure every other new mother has gone through what I'm going through and I just have to stick it out." I gazed down at Ryder and gently rocked him.

"You're a bad liar, Callie. I have a feeling I know what it is but you'll just lie to me again. Just know this, you are a beautiful woman and are going to be an awesome mother. What you're feeling could be post-partum or it could be just old fashioned insecurity but whatever it is, you need to admit it before you can get help."

I grew angry. "Jane, you are my friend and I expect a little more support than criticism. You don't have a direct line to my psyche so quit trying to analyze me."

She stepped back and held up her hands. "I'm not trying to analyze you, I want to help you. I went through the same exact thing as you when I had Jolene but I didn't have a gorgeous husband to validate me and make me feel better about myself. Obviously, you're going to use this anger as a shield, but you're not going to run me off. I'm here for you. I'm family."

I started to speak but then felt a sob hitch in my throat. "I...I..." I couldn't say how I was feeling. It was all jammed up inside me. Jane didn't say a word. She wrapped her arms around me and held me tight. I felt the tears begin to flood down my cheeks.

I heard Jane call out to Jay and he came into the kitchen. Jane let me go and I saw why Jane had fallen in love with him. With complete understanding, he smiled and reached for Ryder. Wordlessly, I lay Ryder in his arms and he took the bottle that Jane handed him. "Don't worry, Callie," he said as he turned to leave, "Jolene and I have got this."

After he left, Jane wrapped her arms around me again. "Let it out, Callie. I know you want to." Within moments I was sobbing. All of the pain and anxiety of motherhood rose up along with my insecurities. "I know you feel bad for feeling this way," Jane said softly, "but it's perfectly normal to be overwhelmed when you become a mom. I've been there and it's not a great place to be."

I sniffled and grabbed a paper towel to blow my nose. "I feel so bad because I love Ryder so much and yet I've got all these other freaking things rolling through my mind. I should be focused on him not my own damn insecurities."

"Well, you're a strong woman Callie but you're also caught in a hormonal tornado. You've got to realize it's really beyond your control. As time goes on, it will get easier but until then, you just need to focus on your beautiful baby."

I heard the front door open as Justin came in. He came straight to the kitchen with the groceries and caught me trying to cover up that I'd been crying. "What happened? Is everything okay with the baby?" He said in a panic.

Jane spoke first. "Callie's just going through the normal mommy phases after having the baby." She hugged me close. "She's going to be just fine."

Justin looked at Jane closely then at me. "Are you sure you're okay? Where's Ryder?"

"Jay's got him," Jane said pointing to the living room. "He and Jolene are giving him a bottle."

Justin put down the bags and as Jane let me go, he gathered me into his arms. I could feel the tension gradually easing as he held me. I heard Jane leave us and I looked up into Justin's crystal blue eyes. "I'm so sorry I'm a blubbering mess," I said softly.

"Baby, why didn't you tell me you were feeling this way? I'm here for you, we're in this together." He cupped my face and wiped the tears away with his thumb.

"Justin, I've been thinking I was being unreasonable. My thoughts really aren't my own right now. All I can think about is how fat I am now and that you won't want anything to do with me."

He tucked his index finger under my chin so I couldn't look away. "Baby, you are the most beautiful woman I've ever laid eyes on. The fact that you are the mother of MY baby makes you even sexier. I wish I could convince you how turned on I am right now being this close to you. Ah, hell…" He pulled me in tight and gave me the most passionate kiss I could ever remember. I felt my body melting into his and I wanted him so badly I couldn't breathe. He pulled away and without breaking his gaze said, "This was just a preview. When Dr. Davidson gives you the okay, it's on!"

I kissed him softly and whispered, "Thank you for being so wonderful. I don't know what I did to deserve you but I'm glad I did it. I love you."

He put his arm around me and walked me out to the living room. Seated on the couch, Jay had Ryder on his shoulder gently rubbing to get him to burp. We walked over and sat down and Jolene ran over to me. "Aunt Callie! He's so cute! When can he play with me?" She said giggling.

"Well he's not ready to play yet but before you know it he'll be following you everywhere," I said laughing. Jolene sat down between Justin and me. "Aunt Callie, your tummy's all gone," she said looking at me closely. "You're all skinny now." Justin's eyes met mine above her head and he gave me a wink.

"Yes, she is Jolene. I was just telling her how good she looks," he said putting his hand on my shoulder and giving me a squeeze.

The intercom buzzed and Justin hopped up to get it. I heard my mom's voice and heard him open the door for her. She came breezing in with Tony trailing behind her. She saw everyone sitting there but ignored us all to head straight to Ryder. Jay must have guessed her intentions because he handed him over to her right away. She rocked him and cooed then seemed to finally notice me. "So, Callie…are you not feeling well? You don't look so good."

My face grew hot as I felt the tears welling up. "I'm fine, Mom. I just had a baby. I think I'm allowed an off day." Out of the corner of my eye, I saw Justin tensing up and knew he wasn't happy. My mom saw my reaction and walked over and kissed me on the forehead. "I'm so proud of you, sweetie. I know I don't have a filter sometimes but I think you're an amazing woman and are going to be a fantastic mother."

I looked up at my mom and smiled. "Thank you for that. I've probably never needed that more than right now."

She went over and sat in the rocking chair and I heard her softly singing to Ryder.

"So, Jane, have you made any wedding plans yet? I'm so excited for you both," I said smiling. I saw Justin relax as my mother got drawn into the conversation.

"Wedding? You've set a date? Oh Jane, how exciting! Have you picked a venue yet? How about a dress? I have a friend who makes spectacular wedding cakes."

Jane smirked as she looked at me and an unspoken 'I love you' passed between us. "Yes, Leslie. Jay and I've set the date. I have picked a venue and we're going to get married in the same chapel Callie and Justin were married in. They just happened to have an opening the day we wanted."

"Oh Jane, that's so awesome!" I said my mood lifting. "What can I do to help?"

"Nothing yet, Cal. I've got everything under control so far. I did plan your wedding, remember? I've got it going on in the wedding planning department. I just called in my connections from yours," she said laughing.

Jay smiled and put his arm around her. "I want her to have her dream wedding so if you can think of anything special she'd like, let me know," he said with a wink.

"Oh, Callie, I forgot to tell you the biggest news of all," Jane said excitedly. "My mom and dad are coming." She started laughing when she saw the shock on my face.

"Your parents? When did this happen? Oh my God, Jane. This is epic news!" I squealed and jumped up to hug her.

"I know, right? They thought I was still with Tyler and heard about his accident, somehow. They called me at work, we started talking and now they are going to come out for the wedding. We Skyped with them last night and they saw Jolene for the first time."

I looked at Jolene who was sitting beside my mom helping her hold the bottle and my heart melted. Despite my mom's wacky ways, I was blessed to have her. Ryder would be spoiled by his grandma and she would be a huge part of his life. I never realized how hard it must have been for Jane having no support from her family. "Well, I'm excited they're coming and if I can help you do anything, please let me help you. I mean it."

"I know you do but you just worry about taking care of that baby and yourself." She gave me a little wink at the end and I knew what she meant.

"Mama?" Jolene asked. "Can I hold Ryder?" I saw concern come over Jane's face and I immediately took control.

"Jolene, if you sit on the couch and behave like a big girl, I'll put Ryder in your lap and you can hold him for a little while." I got up and took Ryder from my mom and watched as Jolene settled herself securely on the couch. Justin grabbed some throw pillows and set them next to her and then I carefully settled Ryder in her arms. She looked down at him and then back up at us.

"He's so heavy!" She sat staring at him watching his lips move as if still sucking on his bottle. "He's neat," she said smiling at each of us. "Can I have one of these too?"

I burst out laughing as I watched Jane's face flush bright red and Jay shifted in his seat. I raised my eyebrows and just had to stir the pot. "Well, can she?"

Jane looked at me, grinned and shook her head. "Jolene, we were just talking about a puppy...now you want a baby?"

I had to smile. The thought of Jane having a baby so close in age to Ryder made me so happy. Jay gave me a little wink and I realized this "baby" was a definite possibility. I was going to have to investigate this further when I could get Jane alone.

****

Justin

I had been watching Callie closely since we brought Ryder home from the hospital and it was worrying me. I noticed she'd been trying on some clothes that she'd worn before she got pregnant and then just balled them up and threw them back in the closet. I'd tried to talk to her but she would happen to hear the baby and need to check on him, so I didn't push it. The insecurities had started long ago and now they had become foremost in her mind again. After a week at home with her, she finally told me that I needed to go to work and that she'd be fine by herself.   I went across the hall before I left and asked Mrs. Callahan to check on her during the day and she assured me she would. I texted her in case they were napping and would hear back from her sporadically during the day. I got home and was coming up the stairs when I heard "Pssst!" I saw Mrs. Callahan's door was cracked open. "Pssst! Come here,

Justin." I walked over, the door flew open and I was yanked inside. She shut the door and looked out the peephole. "Good, she didn't see you."

"What's going on?" I said looking down at the poodle sniffing my shoes.

"I've got a Callie update," she whispered. "This morning after you left, she put Ryder in his little car carrier and set him by the door. She then started running up and down the stairs like a madwoman. I don't think that's a good thing to be doing since she just had the baby."

I stood there stunned. She was working out and the doctor had specifically told her not to do any strenuous exercise until she went back for her checkup. I patted Mrs. Callahan on the shoulder. "Thank you for telling me. I appreciate your watching her for me."

"Anytime. I love you kids and don't want anything to happen to either of you," she said squeezing my arm.

I headed to the door and looked out to see if the coast was clear. Callie hadn't seen me so I scooted out the door to the stairs. I stomped my feet so she'd know I was coming and she opened the door with a smile. She gave me a kiss and I noticed she'd just gotten out of the shower. "So, how was your day with Ryder?" I asked hoping she wouldn't lie to me.

"Great, we slept and ate all day. Pretty boring stuff." She looked away and I saw she was hiding the truth.

"You didn't do anything strenuous, I hope. You know the doctor said no major stuff until he checks you out." I was giving her the out and hoping she'd take it.

"No, absolutely not. I lay on the couch all day unless I was feeding our hungry boy. Oh, I think I just heard him stirring." She picked up the baby monitor and listened closely. I didn't hear a thing but she smiled and said, "Yep, there he is, right on time."

I was so tempted to say I knew better, but I didn't want to start an argument. She'd gotten defensive every time I mentioned she wasn't eating much, and I was very careful to tread lightly around her knowing this could be post-pregnancy hormone wackiness. I was also concerned because of her past insecurities about her body and knew I'd have to be observant but stealth about it.

"So, what do you feel like for dinner tonight, babe?" I called out. I heard her shuffling around in Ryder's room so I picked up the baby monitor. I could hear her talking to Ryder very quietly.

"Your daddy wants to make me eat but I can't eat too much because I need to get into my clothes again. You understand, don't you, little man?"

My heart broke when I heard her say those words and it hurt that she couldn't say them to me. I'd bent over backwards to show her how beautiful and sexy she was, but she was convinced she wasn't.

She walked out of the nursery, saw me holding the baby monitor and stopped. "Um, what are you doing with that?" She asked nervously.

I looked at the monitor in my hand and sighed, "Listening…just listening."

"Justin, I can explain…" she began.

"Babe, there isn't anything you need to explain. You feel fat and horrible and no matter what I say, you won't believe me." I turned and grabbed my keys. "I'm going to get something to eat. If you want something, text me." I knew it was wrong to walk out on her, but I'd had enough. I slammed the door behind me and saw Mrs. Callahan peek out the door, but I kept going down the stairs until I got to my car. When I got there I took a deep breath and tried to calm down but it kept replaying in my mind. As I was getting in my car, I glanced up at the window and could see Callie holding Ryder. I almost went back up, but I knew that it was better to walk away than let this escalate into something neither of us could take back. I drove over to Jay's house and pulled into the driveway. I didn't get out, just sat there trying to get my head together. I heard a knock on my window and looked up to see Jane standing there, arms folded.

I rolled down the window and she leaned in. "What in the hell are you guys doing?" She said poking me in the shoulder.

"I'm assuming she called you," I said laying my head back on the headrest.

"She called. She was crying so hard I couldn't understand her at first. I thought something had happened to you or Ryder and I was a second away from freaking out." She reached down, unlocked the door and opened it. "You're coming inside. We need to talk about this."

I climbed out and followed her into the house. Jay was sitting on the couch and stood as I came in. "So, what's happening, my friend?" He said slapping me on the back.

"I need to know what she told you. So far, she's lied to me," I said dropping onto the couch.

Jane sat next to me and placed her hand on my arm. "She told me that she's been dieting and exercising behind your back and that tonight you caught her on the monitor saying it out loud."

"Well, she told you more than she told me. Mrs. Callahan saw her running up and down the stairs today and I've noticed she eats about three bites of her dinner every night and I doubt she's eating during the day. I'm really worried about her, Jane. I love her and don't want her to get sick. She's beautiful just the way she is and she won't accept that."

Jane leaned forward and met me eye to eye. "Justin, she's had this problem her entire life. Ashley is probably the main reason she is like she is. They were friends from way back and Callie told me she always felt inferior to her. She never felt beautiful because everyone noticed Ashley first. Yes, her mom doesn't help boost her confidence but truthfully, I think it's going back to Ashley."

I sat there and thought of all the encounters that I'd had with Ashley and I could totally see her overshadowing Callie with her all-about-me attitude. The funny thing was that I'd never looked at Ashley that way, at all. She was superficial and shallow and that was not attractive in my book. Her beauty was bought and Callie's was all natural. I loved how Callie looked in the morning when she first woke up, hair disheveled and blanket marks on her face. She was beautiful when she was pregnant and she is beautiful now.

"Jane, what can I do to make it better? I don't want to fight but if she's going to lie to me, I can't handle that. We have to have trust. We both had trust issues when we were dating when she got the wrong impression of Ashley and I and I thought she was dating Jay." I looked over at Jay who laughed out loud.

"Wow, you were wrong on that one!" Jay said leaning back in his chair.

"I know, and I'm thankful my dad worked it out for me but he can't do it this time. I need to handle this one on my own. Is she okay, Jane?"

"She'll be okay, but I have to tell you this, she's being hit with a hormonal tidal wave right now and it is magnified by her own insecurities. I know she's not feeling attractive and her body has been through a lot of changes that she feels you won't find desirable."

I sat there dumbfounded. "How could that be possible? I've loved her from the moment I saw her at that conference and I was so intrigued by my dad's description of her that I felt something before I even met her. It was an instant attraction for me and it's never changed. When we were going through our misunderstandings phase, I never stopped thinking of her and wanting to kill Jay." I looked at Jay and laughed. "Sorry, but I really did."

Jay laughed along with me. "No harm, no foul, friend. She's a beautiful woman and it's easy to understand why you'd think there was a line of guys dying to take your place."

"Then why can't she see that?" I asked, throwing my hands up.

Jane shook her head. "Justin, women are very complex. There is no explanation for why we act as wacky as we do just like there's no explanation for you guys either," she said gesturing to Jay and I.

Jay and I looked at each other sheepishly and nodded. "You're right, baby," Jay said winking at Jane.

I took a deep breath and stood up. "Well, I guess it's time to be a grown-up and quit running away from stuff when it gets too intense."

I hugged Jane, shook Jay's hand and left their house. On the way home, I stopped at the store and grabbed a big bouquet of brightly colored flowers. When I pulled up at the condo, I could see just a dim light in the window but Callie wasn't standing there. Grabbing the flowers, I went up the stairs and quietly unlocked the door. She was lying on the couch asleep with Ryder in his Pack 'n Play beside her. I knelt down and kissed her softly on the lips. Her eyes fluttered open and immediately I saw her bottom lip begin to quiver. "Hey beautiful," I said softly. She started to sit up, but I gently pushed her back against the throw pillow. "I want to tell you how sorry I am for the way I behaved tonight. I ran away when I should have stayed here and talked it out." She started to speak, but I put my finger to her lips and I saw her bite her bottom lip. "I love you Callie. I love you more than you could ever know. I know words won't convince you but I'm going to try anyway. I can remember the first time I saw you like it was yesterday. When I walked in the room, I didn't know where you were going to be sitting but my eyes found you right away. There wasn't anyone else in the room as far as I was concerned. Your smile lit up the room and when I sat down next to you, I was so nervous but you jumped right in to defend my dad's seat." She chuckled a little at that but I still saw tears welling in her eyes. "Every moment since the first one has been precious to me. I haven't looked at another woman and I won't because when I promised to love you to the end of our days, I meant it."

She took a deep hitching breath and then blew it out. "I sat here after you left with all my crazy thoughts swirling around in my head and one kept coming to me…I love you and I don't want to lose you." I saw a tear slip down her cheek and I brushed it away. "All my life I've felt inferior and Justin, let's face it…you're gorgeous. I've never understood why you chose me, but I'm thankful you did."

I brushed back the hair from her beautiful hazel eyes. "I'm the lucky one, Cal. I found my soulmate and together we've made a miracle. Do you think Ryder has any faults?" I slid the Pack 'n Play over closer to us. She looked down at our sleeping angel and shook her head.

"No, he's perfect," she said blinking back tears.

"Well he's made up of both of us and that's what makes him perfect." I touched his cheek and his lips moved in a sucking motion. He stirred but didn't wake.

"Oh Justin, I've been such an idiot. Why do I let things get into my head?" She said throwing her head back down on the pillow.

I leaned over her and looked down into her eyes. "You've been this way a long time but I've got a lifetime to fix you. I'm going to show you every day as many times as you'll let me. The only way to make you see how much I want you is to show you in every way possible."

She chuckled. "Well, you'll be a busy man in about five weeks if that's your plan."

"Oh baby, we can still go to bed and make out. I intend on giving you my preview of the coming attractions." She smiled and I saw the Callie I knew and loved looking back at me.

Chapter 9

Jane

I was surprised to get a call from the court saying that they had accepted the petition for Tyler to terminate his parental rights. Apparently, the judge felt that since he was voluntarily giving them up without any resistance from me that it was in the best interest of Jolene to fast track them through. I walked into the bedroom and slipped my arms around Jay's bare chest as he stood shaving for work. "The court's accepting the paperwork and it will be finalized within a few days." I rested my head against his back and hugged him tightly. "They said Tyler will still be responsible for Jolene's support unless she's adopted and has two parents to support her."

Jay spun around to face me. "Well that won't be long because I want to get the paperwork started for the adoption as soon as we're married."

"Jolene loves you so much and it would make everything perfect." I grabbed his face which was still covered in shaving cream and gave him a big kiss.

He broke into a huge grin. He turned back to the sink and finished shaving. "I want to give her the ring she wanted and we'll explain that we're making our family official."

"I think that's a wonderful idea. I love you so much." I gave him a little squeeze on the butt and started to walk away when he grabbed me and pulled me back.

He kissed me, and I could feel him rubbing the shaving cream he had left on my face. I squealed and tried to pull away but he held me until I was breathless from laughing. Finally, he let me go, and I looked in the mirror and saw what I looked like. I started laughing even harder and grabbed a wash cloth to wipe it off. "Mr. Anderson, you've been a bad boy!"

He grabbed a towel and quickly wiped his face. I heard him growl and say, "I know I've never told you this but I love it when you call me Mr. Anderson." He grabbed me and pulled me against him. His lips came down on mine, and I wrapped my arms around his neck and stroked his hair.

"Mama?" We broke apart a moment before Jolene came bounding into the bathroom. "You were laughing and I want to see what's funny."

Jay smiled, turned to the sink and squeezed a tiny bit of shaving cream onto his finger. He spun around and plopped it right on her nose. Her mouth flew open as she looked down and started giggling. "Daddy! What did you do?"

"I wanted to show you what we were laughing at. Your mom just had some on her face too," he said rinsing off his hand.

"I wanna see!" She said jumping up and down, shaving cream flying off of her nose. He reached down and swiped some off her nose and smeared it on mine! Jolene was in hysterics. He seemed pretty proud of himself for catching me off guard and was distracted enough that he never saw me take the can of shaving cream and squirt it on his head.

"Someone's gonna need another shower," I said laughing. He had to laugh too. He shook his head and the shaving cream flew all over the bathroom.

"Gotcha!" He said laughing.

We all grabbed towels and started wiping up the mess and I heard my phone chime. I left Jay and Jolene to finish cleaning up and went to grab my phone which was now showing a missed call and voice mail from a number I didn't know. I started listening to the message and heard Tyler's voice.

"Hey Jane, it's me, Tyler. I just wanted to call to tell you that I'm being discharged in the morning and I'm going to be heading back to Portland. I was wondering if you could do me a favor before I go and if you don't want to, I totally understand. Would you bring Jolene to see me? I promise I won't tell her who I am but I just want to meet her the right way. Give me a call back and let me know what you think."

Jay and Jolene walked out of the bathroom and saw me standing with the phone. "What's up, babe?" Jay asked.

"Jolene, honey…would you run and get me your hairbrush so I can do your hair?" I asked needing to have a moment alone with Jay.

"Okay, I'll be right back!" She said running out of the room.

I looked to make sure she was out of earshot and I said in a low whisper, "Tyler's leaving town and he wants to see Jolene."

Jay looked at me and shrugged his shoulders. "Why not. He's signed the papers and he's leaving town. I don't see why he can't see her."

I felt so relieved because I'd immediately thought the same thing. "Jay, you're an amazing man. I love you."

"I'm only amazing because I'm with you," he said kissing me lightly on the lips.

"So we take Jolene this evening, then?" I asked getting ready to call Tyler back.

He was tying his tie and stopped to look at me with surprise. "We? You want me to go with you?"

"Go where, Daddy?" Jolene interrupted.

Jay looked down at Jolene and said, "Do you remember how we talked about the friend who was in the hospital and he was very sick?" Jolene nodded. "Well, he's doing much better now and we're going to visit him tonight before he goes back home."

"Yay! I prayed for him! Can we take him a balloon? I can draw him a picture!" She said bouncing around.

I looked at her and smiled. "Sure, baby. We can get him a balloon and when you're at daycare today you can draw him a picture."

"Okay, Mama, maybe I'll draw him my puppy," she said walking back out of the bedroom.

Jay looked at me and started laughing. "She hasn't forgotten that puppy has she?" He grabbed his phone and pulled up his calendar. "We'll try looking next weekend. How does that sound?"

"Sounds great to me," I said smiling. "She's going to be one happy little girl."

Jay wrapped his arm around me and pulled me close. "I can't wait to give you both everything you've ever wanted or needed."

"Jay, you're all we need," I said cupping his face. I gave him another kiss before we headed to get Jolene ready and out the door.

We dropped her off at daycare and I heard her tell Miss Torri that she had a very special picture to draw. We spent the day Skyping with Callie about some design changes we needed that only she could do and I got to see Ryder. We told her about Tyler's request to see Jolene and that we were going by the hospital after work. Jay left the room for a moment and I asked Callie if everything was okay at home. She knew that Justin had come over to our place that night and I really just wanted to check in on them and make sure things were better.

Callie said in a whisper, "Can Jay hear me?"

I looked across the office and saw him pulling some plans from the file drawers so I knew he'd be a little while. I shook my head no. She grinned and waggled her eyebrows. "Oh Jane, things are so good. Justin brought me flowers that night and made me feel so special. I promised him I wouldn't exercise and diet without talking to my doctor first and then we moved our conversation to the bedroom. Let's just say, my man rocks!" She closed her eyes and sighed. "I'm such a lucky woman."

I had to giggle. I whispered, "Well, he's a lucky man too. You guys are awesome together and look at that gorgeous baby you made."

I looked over to see Jay coming back to the office so I let Callie know I'd talk to her later. "Jane, thank you for being so good to both of us. I love you, sis."

I smiled. "That's what family does!"

We said our goodbyes and I saw it was almost time to pick up Jolene to go to see Tyler. I felt a knot in my stomach because I really didn't know how this was going to go but I just prayed for the best. We arrived at daycare to find Jolene waiting with her special picture which surprisingly was not a puppy but an angel. Her angel had stick legs and arms, a crooked halo and big purple wings but it was definitely an angel. Smiling, I took the paper and cupped her face. "Sweetie, this is really pretty. I think he's going to like this a lot."

"Can we go get a balloon for him, too? Can I have one, too? I promise I won't pop it," she said excitedly.

Jay picked her up and sat her in the car. "Slow down, Sweet Pea. We'll get the balloon and I think we can get you one, too."

"Yay!" She bounced up and down. "Daddy can we play Kidz Bop?"

"Sure," he said climbing in. I looked at him and laughed.

"What? The songs are pretty good!" he said winking at me.

We bopped to Kidz Bop and I even heard Jay singing along and my face actually hurt from smiling and laughing. It eased my nervousness and after we'd gotten the balloons we headed to the hospital.

As we got closer to the room, Jay stopped. Confused, I looked at him and said, "What's wrong?"

He touched my arm gently and softly said, "I think you both need to do this without me." I started to protest, but he kissed me gently. "Jane, this is the last time he'll see Jolene for who knows how long. Let him have this memory. I have no problem with it."

I looked at Jay and I felt tears prickling my eyes. "Jay, thank you." He just nodded and kissed me again. I knelt in front of Jolene and got her attention away from the balloon she was gazing at. "Sweetie, I need to tell you that the friend we're visiting is Mr. Tyler. Do you remember him?" She nodded so I continued. "Do you remember that I told you he wasn't my friend? Well, we are friends again and he wanted to meet you and tell you goodbye before he moves far away."

She nodded and grinned. "I hope he likes the angel I drew him. I think he needs an angel." Standing up, I looked at Jay and shook my head in disbelief. My child was amazing! Clutching her drawing, I took her hand and with her holding the balloon we knocked and went into Tyler's room.

Tyler was sitting in a chair by the window reading a book. He looked really good and only had a few bandages showing. He glanced up as we came in and smiled.

"Hey, Jane. Hello, Jolene," he said quietly.

Jolene hid behind me slightly as I walked in. She peeked around me and then hid again. I wanted to make her feel comfortable so I said, "Hi Tyler! How are you doing? Feeling better?"

He took his cue from me and smiled. "Yes, I am! I'm almost as good as new." I could feel Jolene's tight grip start to slacken.

"Well we've got some things to make you feel better! We brought you a 'Get Well' balloon. Jolene, do you want to show him his balloon?"

She stepped from behind me. "It's to make you feel better," she said shyly.

"Oh wow! It's really big! How are you holding that big balloon without flying away?" He said wide-eyed and grinning.

"I'm a big girl," she said. "I drew you a picture, too."

I held out the picture to Tyler and watched as he took it. "Jolene, this is perfect," he said emotionally.

"It's an angel," she said walking a little closer to him. "See, she has wings. I made them purple 'cause I like purple."

"I see that! They are beautiful! Is she going to keep me safe?" He asked smiling.

"Yes, she's gonna fly over you and make sure you don't get sick anymore," she said walking over to stand by his chair.

I watched as they talked together and my emotions were overwhelming me. I saw glimpses of the Tyler I'd known and loved. He looked up at me and smiled. "Hey Jane, someone brought me a teddy bear this morning but I don't have room in my suitcase for it. Do you know anyone who might want to give him a home?"

Jolene's eyes lit up and I saw her look at me with wide eyes. I had to stifle a laugh. "Um, gosh Tyler, let me think." Jolene was now actively trying to get my attention by bouncing on the balls of her feet and clapping her hands together. I couldn't make her suffer anymore. "You know Tyler, Jolene has some teddy bears and she takes really good care of them. You may want to ask her if she would mind taking care of one more."

I saw the look of excitement in her eyes as she looked at him, waiting for his response. He pointed to his bed where I saw a sizeable lump under the covers. "There you go, Jolene. He's all yours!"

She ran over to the bed and pulled back the blanket to reveal a beautiful plush teddy bear that had to be almost two feet tall. She squealed and grabbed it by the hand pulling it over to give it a big hug. "Oh he's cute!" She said turning to show me. "Look Mama! He's almost as big as me!"

He really was! I had to laugh at her struggling to carry him over to show me. I took him from her and sat him on the end of the bed. I looked at his tag. "It says his name is Maxie. What do you say, baby?"

"Thank you, Mr. Tyler! I promise I'll take care of him." Tyler smiled as she threw her arms around his shoulders. "Guess what? My daddy's gonna take me to get a puppy of my very own too!"

I saw a fleeting shadow cross Tyler's face but he quickly recovered. "That's awesome! Have you picked out a name for your puppy yet?" He asked watching her with a smile.

"Well, I was gonna call it Puppy but then Miss Torri at my daycare said it won't be a puppy when he grows up so I'm gonna call him Spongebob," she said seriously.

Laughing, I asked, "What if he is a she?"

"Oh, hmm…then I'd call her Angel."

Tyler and I both exchanged a look and I nodded. "Those are both fine names," I said. I looked at the time and realized it was getting late. "Well, baby, tell Mr. Tyler goodbye and we'll let him get some rest."

She smiled and hugged him again. "Bye, Mr. Tyler." He patted her on the head and I saw tears welling up but he quickly blinked them back.

"Jolene, I hope you'll be a good girl for your mom and dad, okay?" He said watching her walk to stand beside me. I picked up the teddy bear and walked over to give Tyler a quick hug.

"Goodbye, Tyler," I said softly.

"Goodbye, Jane and thank you," he said grasping my hand. "And please thank Jay for me too." I smiled and nodded.

We walked out and as we got to the lobby, Jay saw us approaching and stood. He saw the teddy bear and smiled. "Who's your new friend, Sweet Pea?" He said reaching down to scoop Jolene up into a big hug.

"His name is Maxie and I'm gonna take care of him for Mr. Tyler," she said breathlessly as he set her back down. She held out her hands for the teddy bear and she gave it a big hug.

"Well, Maxie is very handsome and I'm sure he's going to love staying in your room," he said taking my hand and pulling me in for a kiss. "You okay?" He whispered in my ear.

I nodded and smiled. "Let's go home and show Maxie around." We walked out of the hospital hand in hand.

****

Jay

Tyler left town and I breathed a sigh of relief. It wasn't that I didn't trust him, I just didn't trust him. Jane had gotten his address and we decided to give him periodic updates about Jolene to be civil. It was finally the weekend and we'd decided today was the day to go puppy hunting. I woke up early, hating to unwrap myself from a deeply sleeping Jane, but I needed to get everything ready before Jolene got up. Funny, it felt like Christmas morning for me with my running around to set everything up for her when she woke. I'd bought a leash, a harness, dog bowl and assorted toys and I took them into her room. She was sleeping peacefully, so I quietly placed the items around her on the bed. I tiptoed back out and went to make some coffee and get some breakfast started. I flipped on the television and watched Spongebob for a while until I heard an ear-splitting shriek.

"DADDY!!!!" She squealed.

I smiled to myself and walked toward her room. Jane was stumbling out tying her robe looking at me with a 'what the hell' look and I just grinned. I walked past her and she followed me to Jolene's room.

"I'M GETTING MY PUPPY!" She said bouncing on her bed.

"Yes ma'am. Today's the day!" I said grabbing her before she bounced completely off the bed onto the floor. I really didn't want to have to spend 'puppy day' at the ER. As soon as her feet hit the floor, she was in the closet pulling out her clothes. Within a few minutes, she was chasing her mom around with the hairbrush and Jane was forced to move into high gear. I poured a cup of coffee for her and handed it off as she passed by. In what seemed like record time, we were all ready and lined up at the door.

"Jolene, Jane…are we prepared? Checklist. Leash, check. Harness, check. Puppy picture folder, check. Looks like we're ready to roll out."

We bundled into the car and drove to the local humane society. I'd done a little research online before we went and knew they had certain procedures before you could adopt, but I was confident that the shelter was the right place to find her new puppy. When we arrived, we were greeted by an adoption counselor whose name was Carolyn and we were shown around. She asked us questions related to our needs and we narrowed down the choices so we didn't overwhelm Jolene. We were seated in a room and one at a time, they brought the puppies in. I was expecting Jolene to pick the first one they brought in, or every one they brought in, but she was very serious and I marveled at how maturely she was handling this for her age. Jane and I were also considering the expected size and weight of the dog knowing this was something we needed to keep in mind. One dog in particular caught Jolene's eye and she played with it more than any other. It was a female Lab mix and she was already six months old. She wasn't very big and Carolyn explained that indicated she wasn't going to become huge. She was very playful but gentle and Jolene sat on the floor and petted and brushed her. When Carolyn began to pick her up to put her back, I saw the look on Jolene's face. "Sweet Pea? Is this the one?" I asked knowing the answer.

Tears brimming, she nodded, "I want her. Please, Daddy?"

I looked up at Carolyn and said, "I think we have our puppy." I also stifled a laugh because she didn't look anything like the puppy pictures Jolene had painstakingly drawn. That's the beauty of finding your soul mate. You never know when you're going to fall in love but you know it when you do. Jane glanced at me and it was like she was reading my mind. She blew me a little kiss and I grinned and caught it. Jolene looked at me and then her mom and giggled. "Now, do we have a name for this puppy, Jolene?"

"Yes, Daddy! I'm gonna call her Angel." She was still petting the puppy that had now fallen asleep beside her leg.

Carolyn then walked us through the adoption process. Angel was going to get a thorough check up with the veterinarian for any shots she might need and also microchipped. Jolene listened as Carolyn explained everything and she said, "Does Angel come home with me today?"

"No, honey," Carolyn explained. "She's going to go to the veterinarian first but it won't take long to get everything done. You can probably pick her up on Monday."

I braced myself for the onslaught of tears but Jolene just nodded. "Okay."

Jane must've been expecting it too because she looked at Jolene with surprise. "Baby, I tell you what. We'll take a picture of Angel so you can show everyone and before you know it, it'll be time to pick her up."

Jolene's face lit up. "Yay! I can show Aunt Callie and Uncle Justin!"

We finished with the adoption and walked back out to the car. As I helped Jolene into the car, she looked at me and said, "Daddy the other puppies don't have homes, do they?"

"No, Sweet Pea. They're waiting for someone to come and take them home just like Angel."

"Daddy, I'm so lucky I got her. Can she sleep in my room?"

"We'll see. She's a puppy and will need a lot of care. Your mom and I will make that decision when we see how she does, okay?"

"Okay. Daddy, I love you and Mama so much!"

My heart melted. "And we love you so much. So, what're we listening to on the way home?"

"KIDZ BOP!" Jolene said waving her hands in the air.

"Kidz Bop, it is!" I said laughing. Jane and I sang along with Jolene as we made our way back to the house.

Chapter 10

Callie

The days were flying by and Ryder was growing bigger every day. After Justin and I had our talk, I quit focusing on my weight and more on my baby. I knew he was right and even though sometimes I would be tempted to jump on the scales or skip a meal, I would think about how hurt he would be and I shook it off. Jane's wedding was fast approaching and I asked Justin if he minded spending some time with Ryder so I could get some time with my bestie. He didn't mind at all. In fact, he made plans with Jay to take the kids to the park.

I hadn't really been dressed up since I got home and since I didn't think sweats were appropriate for a girl's day out, I grabbed a pair of my jeans from the closet and slipped them on. When the button closed with no effort and the zipper went up with ease, I realized I'd gotten what I wanted without trying to kill myself in the process. I walked out into the living room where Justin was putting Ryder in the stroller and nonchalantly walked by. I heard a whistle behind me and turned to see Justin totally checking me out.

"Babe, you look amazing!" He said with a huge grin.

I returned the smile. "I feel pretty amazing," I said grabbing a bottle of water from the fridge. I walked over and knelt in front of the stroller. "Now you be a good boy for Daddy, okay?" He cooed and waved his little fists in the air. I had to laugh. I loved how every day he was doing something new. He was also sleeping most of the night which had improved my mood more than I realized.

"Jane and I are going to get her dress fitted and grab a coffee. I shouldn't be too long but if you need me, call, okay?" I said as I grabbed my keys.

"Sure, but we'll be fine. Did you hear Mommy, Ryder? She thinks we can't handle a day out. We'll show her!" He said in a goofy voice.

I shook my head and walked out laughing. Mrs. Callahan was coming up the stairs with a man who appeared to be her age. "Hey, Callie. Have you got a minute?" She asked.

I glanced at my watch. "I just have about five to spare," I said with a smile.

"Callie, I'd like to introduce my boyfriend, Marvin," she said gesturing to the man.

He bowed his head and extended his hand. "Nice to meet you, Callie."

"Well, it's nice to meet you too, Marvin. How long have you two been going out?" I asked.

He put his arm around Mrs. Callahan and hugged her. "Actually my son introduced us. He escorted Mary to your wedding and a few days later invited the both of us out to dinner together but conveniently had to leave within a few minutes. We talked for hours and have been inseparable since."

I looked at Mrs. Callahan in disbelief. "You've been dating all this time and I'm just finding out about it? You sure are sneaky, young lady," I said breaking into a grin.

"Well, you have a lot going on, sweetie and I figured there'd be a right time to introduce you and here we are."

"I'm very happy for you both and I guess I'll be seeing you around Marvin?" I said giving both of them a hug.

Marvin grinned. "Actually, I'm moving in next month. Mary and I decided it was the smart thing to do and I'm over here most of the time anyway. I'm trying to convince her to marry me but she's being pretty stubborn. I told her that when she's ready, she'll have to ask me."

I laughed out loud. "Well, I'd better be one of the first to know."

Mrs. Callahan gazed up at Marvin and smiled. "Don't worry, Callie. He's wearing me down. I'm sure I'll give in before too long."

I giggled and hugged them again. "I'll see you both around then!" I dashed down the stairs, jumped in my car and headed to the bridal shop to meet Jane.

I saw her car already parked outside and hurried in so I wouldn't miss anything. She was speaking with someone when I walked in and when she looked over and saw me she waved me over. "Karla, this is Callie. Callie, Karla is helping me with my dress today."

We nodded and smiled. "Nice to meet you," I said while setting my purse down. "I'm sorry I'm a bit late. We can get started whenever you're ready."

"No worries," Jane said sitting down on a big fluffy couch. "There's another bride being fitted for her gown and then I'm next. I'm willing to wait since she's using the room with the big mirrors." I sat next to her and that's when she noticed. "Callie! You look fabulous! Are those your skinny jeans? Stand up and let me see!"

"Yes, these are the jeans I wore when Justin and I went out on our first date and they were snug then but they fit perfectly now. I think it's all the walking with the stroller that's done it. I promised Justin that I wouldn't make myself sick trying to diet so I just quit thinking about it. Apparently, it worked!"

"Well, I am so proud of you," she said standing to give me a hug.

We were startled to hear a woman's voice yelling from the other room. "I don't care how much it costs, I want the dress I saw when I came in the first time."

We could hear the saleswoman trying to calm the bride to be. "I'm sorry Miss but that dress is spoken for. As a matter of fact, the bride is out in the lobby waiting for her fitting."

"I want that dress!" She shrieked.

Jane and I looked at each other in disbelief. "What a freakin' nutjob," she whispered. I could only nod.

"I want you to go out and offer to give her $1,000 more than the dress costs so I can have it!" She screeched.

Again we heard the saleswoman trying to diffuse the mood. "I'm sorry Miss but she's already paid for the dress and I will not go out and try to buy back a dress from a bride who is happy with her dress," she explained.

"Well if you won't do it, I will!" She yelled.

Jane and I looked at each other with alarm and tried to find a place to disappear. It reminded me of the time we thought Matt Cooper was coming in my office so we hid very conspicuously and it had turned out to be Jay. This time, I found a mirror to scoot behind and Jane buried herself in a rack of dresses.

I couldn't see what was happening but I could hear it. "YOU! Of all people, it's you!" I heard the bride shout.

"Bitch! YOU are the one who wants my dress? It'll be a cold day in Hell!" I heard Jane fire back.

I risked a peek out from behind my obviously awesome hiding place and saw the red hair first. No way. It couldn't be. Jane looked over at me and that's when the redhead turned and I could see it was Ashley. At least I thought it was Ashley. This altered version of Ashley had apparently fallen into a plastic surgeon's office and stayed a while. She now sported the infamous trout pout, a very close replica of the Michael Jackson nose, and her eyebrows were lifted so high she looked like she was permanently surprised. I also noticed she'd enhanced the 'girls' and was probably sporting a DD where she'd more than likely been a C before. She'd put on some weight too. I watched as she looked me up and down and she scrunched up her MJ nose. "Callie. Well, it looks like you had your kid. I guess your stretch marks must be out of this world."

I tilted my head slightly as if puzzled. "Actually, Ashley, I didn't get any stretch marks, come to think of it." Proudly, I pulled up my shirt and the top part of my pants to show her there were none. I'd apparently inherited my good skin from my mother who had no stretch marks either. She sneered as she looked but I could tell it unnerved her. "I guess if anyone would have to be worried about stretch marks, it would be you," I continued. "You have several areas to keep an eye on…lips, boobs, and hips."

I heard Jane snort and Ashley whipped her head around to glare at her. "The last time I saw you, you slapped me and I owe you one." She started to bring her hand back but Jane was faster. She grabbed Ashley's arm and held on tight. "I don't think you want to do that, Ashley," she said looking her right in the eye. "You deserved that slap for being a deliberate bitch and I kinda hoped it would make you grow up but apparently you've kicked your bitch mode into high gear."

Ashley struggled to get her arm free, but Jane held on tight. I could see the employees of the store hovering in the background waiting for it to escalate but Jane held her cool. Between gritted teeth, Ashley snarled, "You are both evil."

Jane looked at her and shook her head. "Ashley, just because your life is screwed up doesn't mean you have to spew venom on everyone else. Oh, and you're NOT getting my dress so you might as well find another one."

Ashley sputtered and wrenched her arm free. She stalked over to me and poked me in the shoulder and threw out one last barb. "I hope your kid looks like you…it'll be just another ugly kid in this world for my future kids to be better than."

I moved so fast I didn't realize it happened but I pushed Ashley with all my might and knocked her over a bench that she was standing beside. As she was falling, she managed to grab my hair, and I returned the favor but ended up standing there with a handful in my hand as her hair extension broke loose. Jane grabbed me from behind and held me back but not before I realized I'd knocked the breath out of her. She stood up and squealed, "You tore out my hair and it costs a lot of money!"

I dropped the hair and backed away. Karla approached us and I grabbed my purse prepared to leave. Instead she walked over to Ashley and asked her to remove herself from the store and to not ever come back.

Ashley snatched her purse from the coat rack, scooped up the hair extension and stomped out the door. Karla then walked over to me and said, "I'm so sorry that happened to you. I'm actually relieved she's gone and I hope you'll stay and help your friend with her wedding gown."

"I made it!" We looked up to see Emily, Jay's mom, come running through the door. "Sorry I'm late, did I miss anything?" Jane and I both burst out laughing realizing just how close we'd come to Jane's future mother-in-law seeing our showdown with Ashley. She and my mom had become BFF's and I didn't need my mom finding out I'd been tussling in the bridal shop. Emily and I were excited to see the dress and make sure it was perfect. Jane went back to the dressing room and slipped it on with Karla's help. We wanted to be surprised so we stayed in the showroom. When she walked out to stand in front of the wall of mirrors I was stunned. She looked truly spectacular. The style of the dress was similar to the one she'd chosen to wear in my wedding. It was sexy with a slit up the front to show her amazing legs and fit her like a glove. In place of a veil, she opted for a simple tiara. Karla handed her a simple bouquet and as she stood under the ambient lighting, I could feel tears springing to my eyes. My best friend was going to marry the man of her dreams and she was glowing with happiness.

I hadn't even begun to think about a dress but Jane had me all fixed up. Karla came from the back carrying a gorgeous navy blue chiffon cocktail length dress paired with a pair of satin pink heels. "I thought you'd like to wear something you can wear again," Jane said holding the dress up in front of me. "This is going to be perfect."

I absolutely loved the dress and that she'd picked it out knowing exactly what my style was. "Jane, it's incredible!" I took it and quickly ran to the dressing room. When I slipped it on, it fit like it was made for me. I slipped on the shoes and the gasps in the room and the smiles told me that I looked pretty good.

As I changed out of the dress, I looked at the time and realized I'd better skip the coffee because Justin had been with the baby for longer than I expected. I looked at my phone and saw no messages or even texts. I gave him a quick call and heard Jolene's giggles in the background. "Hey babe, how are you holding up with Ryder?"

He laughed. "We're doing great. Jolene is swinging on the swing set and Jay and I are hanging on a bench like a couple with Ryder in his stroller and Angel on her leash. We've already had someone ask us how long we've been together."

I could hear Jay in the background laughing as he said, "The funny part was they said the baby looked like me!"

Justin scoffed, "Whatever. Ryder's got my blue eyes!"

Jay countered, "All babies have blue eyes at first…just wait, they'll turn green!"

I listened to them going back and forth and laughed so hard I had tears coming from my eyes. Jane came back to get her things and saw me bent over laughing. "What are you laughing about?" She asked with a puzzled look.

"Our men are a couple now," I managed to squeak out as I covered the phone. "Crap, I'll tell you in a minute." She shrugged her shoulders and started laughing as she walked away. I composed myself. "Do you need me to come relieve you?" I asked sincerely.

"Nah, we're all good. We're getting ready to take Ryder to the bar and get him his first beer. I hear it puts hair on your chest and he's looking really smooth," Justin said laughing again.

"I swear you and Jay together. I never would have believed you could be this comical. You should go on the road with this act," I said sarcastically.

"Well, then we'd really get the rumors flying. I'd rather stay home and cuddle with my totally hot wife," he said in an overly manly voice.

"I second that," I heard Jay yell.

"Well, if you boys are okay, Jane and I are going to take Emily to the coffee shop for a quick caffeine hit. I love you babe…please behave," I said smiling.

"You got it! Jay, quit putting your arm around me. I gotta go. He's making things worse now." Our call ended and I grabbed my purse and met up with Jane and Emily out in the lobby.

****

Jane

The week before the wedding, I was an absolute nut. My parents were flying in on Thursday and I was a nervous wreck about seeing them again. Monday was unreal at work and when I picked up Jolene from daycare, she came home and began throwing up. I hated seeing my baby so sick and eventually she exhausted herself and fell asleep. Angel slept right beside her on the bed and I didn't move her because it was so sweet. I knew that if she hadn't improved by morning I'd have to take her to the doctor but the next morning, she hopped out of bed as usual with Angel in tow and wanted breakfast because, as she put it, "Mama, I'm starving!"

I got up to make her something to eat and just looking at the food made me feel sick, so I passed off the cooking duties to Jay and ended up heading to the bathroom myself. Jay came in to check on me and as he wet a washcloth with cold water to dab my head, he told me that he'd called his mom to watch Jolene for the day since she could be carrying a bug. His mom was the anti-bacterial queen and no germ had a chance of getting past her, so I accepted the offer and figured I'd spend the day with a bucket.

After a few hours of being sick, I thought how behind I was going to be with the wedding just three days away so I gathered myself up, got dressed and headed to the doctor's office. I figured they would be able to give me something for the nausea and let me get some final preparations made.

I sat in the doctor's office filling out the paperwork and within a few minutes was taken back to be weighed, pee in a cup and get my temperature taken. The nurse put me in a room and I sat on the paper-covered table with sweat beading on my forehead as I fought the nausea that washed over me again.

Dr. Zelnick walked in and looked at his clipboard. "So, Jane. What brings you here today?"

I could feel my tongue getting that thick feeling right before I got sick, so I quickly told him what had been happening.

"Hmm, so tell me, you've just started feeling this way?" He looked down at his paperwork and started writing and checking little boxes.

"Yes, since this morning. But Dr. Zelnick, I'm getting married Saturday and I can't be sick! I have too much to do!"

He nodded calmly and kept looking at the clipboard. Finally, he said, "You didn't indicate when your last menstrual cycle was. Do you know?"

I shook my head with irritation. "Of course I know. I keep it on my phone calendar." I grabbed my purse and pulled out my phone. I found the calendar and scooted back to the month before. I'd never marked it. I went back to the month before, no mark. I thought for a moment and realized that was about the time I'd started my birth control. "I don't have it marked but I think it's because I'd gone on birth control since I was in a serious relationship and I guess I forgot to write it down."

He nodded and looked back down at the clipboard. "Is there a chance you might be pregnant?" He asked me seriously, and I couldn't help but laugh.

"Well, I guess since I'm sleeping with someone it could be a possibility but again, I am on birth control so that's not an issue. Can't you give me some nausea medicine so I can go get some errands done?"

"Jane, I just have to ask these questions. I'm not trying to upset you," he said taking out the stethoscope and beginning his exam. He made some notes and a few minutes later, I heard a knock at the door. He opened it and the nurse handed him some paperwork. He glanced at it and I heard him sigh. "Well, it seems you're a 1%."

"Excuse me?" I asked confused.

"Oral contraceptives are 99.9% effective so it appears you're in the .1% that it doesn't work. Jane, you're pregnant," he said walking over to put his hand on my shoulder.

I could hear a buzzing in my ears and although I heard what he said, it seemed like it was a dream. Pregnant? I'd never even considered it.

He continued, "I'm guessing you're about six to seven weeks along but I want you to go to your GYN to get a viability ultrasound to determine exactly how far along you are."

I nodded mutely as he wrote out some information and pulled some pamphlets off the rack to give to me. I finally muttered, "I don't know what to say. I'm thrilled but scared at the same time."

"I'm sure you are but that's why I want you to schedule an appointment as soon as possible with your doctor. We want to make sure everything's okay. They'll want to get you on some prenatal vitamins."

"I'll call as soon as I leave here," I promised.

I got my things, checked out and went out to my car. In the silence of the car, I could feel my body trembling and silent tears fell down my cheeks. With shaking hands, I called Callie.

"Hey girl, what's up?" She said cheerfully.

"Callie? I'm pregnant," I blurted.

"What? How do you know?" She asked.

"I just left my doctor. I thought it was a stomach virus but it's a baby." Hearing myself say the words made me shake even more.

"Where are you now? I'll come to you. Justin's home for lunch and he won't mind. He can call into work and stay here with the baby," she said anxiously.

"I'm at Dr. Zelnick's. I'll stay here and wait."

"Be there in ten minutes. Love you. Bye."

Those ten minutes were excruciating because my mind was whirling. I knew my situation was different this time but I was still unmarried and although it was a slim chance Jay would run, there was a chance. I heard Callie's car pull up and she ran to my car. Once she was inside, she reached over and hugged me and we cried together. "Jane, this is a good thing. I know what you're thinking but this is a good thing. Jay loves you and will marry you on Saturday whether you're pregnant or not."

I knew she was right. I needed to get to my OB/GYN as soon as possible to see how things were before I got too carried away. I called my doctor's office and explained what I'd just found out and they told me to come over right away because they had a cancellation. I told Callie I was going over there and she said she was going too. She followed me over to Dr. Gardner's office and the receptionist took me straight back. Callie stayed in the waiting room while they ran the same tests Dr. Zelnick had and they all came back the same, pregnant. They put me into an exam room and within a few minutes, Dr. Gardner came in. "Jane, how are you?" He asked sitting down in a little chair beside the exam table.

I answered honestly. "Freaked out?" He looked at my trembling hands and placed his hand on top to still them.

"I can totally understand your reaction, especially since we'd put you on birth control just a couple of months ago. This happens and unfortunately, this happy event is tainted by your surprise but I think after you let this sink in, you'll be just fine."

I nodded. "We, my fiancé and I, want a baby but this just wasn't planned," I said dropping my gaze.

"Jane, I've been a doctor for twenty-five years and I can't tell you how many times I've heard that but I believe there was a plan…God just let you in on it." He smiled and started plugging in his ultrasound equipment. "Let's see how far along you are."

"Wait! Can my friend Callie come back here? I want her with me."

He nodded and picked up the phone to call for the nurse to bring Callie back. Within a few minutes, she was seated in the little chair and a nurse was standing by to assist Dr. Gardner as he was setting up the ultrasound. I lay back on the table and he began the exam. Within a couple of moments, I heard Callie gasp. "Aww, it's so tiny," she said with wonder.

I couldn't see the monitor but soon I could hear a quick thumping. "Jane, it looks like you're about nine weeks along," he said as he printed a picture for me. I looked at Callie and smiled.

"Are you getting the same déjà vu feeling I am? Weren't we in this same place with a certain little girl on the screen just about five years ago?" She said laughing.

Dr. Gardner took a few more measurements and printed off a really clear picture of our baby who he informed me was the size of a grape. He turned the monitor and I could see the little blip racing across the screen. I felt tears roll down my cheeks. "How am I going to tell Jay? I don't know what to do." I felt fear creeping in again.

Callie got up and walked over to my side. "Why don't you do this…take this picture, put it in a gift bag with some baby goodies and give it to him before the wedding. He deserves to know."

Again, she was right. "I'll do some thinking about this but I know I need to tell him. I just can't help feeling that fear of him leaving me."

She looked at me seriously. "If you give him this before the wedding and he doesn't show up, you'll know. If he does, then you'll have all you've ever dreamed of and more. Either way, you've got a baby on the way and I'll be here to help you because that's what family does."

Dr. Gardner had been listening silently and after Callie finished talking to me, he gave me a list of vitamins to take and told me to schedule another appointment for next month.

I got to my car, gave Callie a hug for being so awesome and headed to Emily's to pick up Jolene.

When I got there, Jolene was watching a movie and Emily was baking some cookies which now smelled amazing to me. She turned from the oven, cocked her head to the side and said, "So what did the doctor say? Flu bug?"

I hesitated and then lied. "Uh, yeah. Flu bug. I'll be fine."

Emily stared at me for a moment then broke into a grin. "You're pregnant, aren't you?

My eyebrows shot up. "Excuse me?" I said laughing.

She walked over to me and gave me a hug. "Woman's intuition. If I'm wrong, that's okay and I'll be disappointed but if I'm right, I want you to know that I'm truly happy for the both of you." I looked at her and then slowly nodded. She hugged me again and we both cried together. "So, when are you going to tell my son?"

We walked over to the kitchen island and I perched on a bar stool. "I was thinking about putting this in a gift basket with some baby goodies," I said pulling the ultrasound picture out of my purse.

Wordlessly, she took the picture and studied it for several minutes. Finally, she said, "I think that's a wonderful idea." We sat and looked at the picture, and I pointed out the baby and told her everything the doctor had said.

We were just getting ready to have a cookie when Jolene came in. "Mama! I didn't know you were here!" She ran over to Emily holding out her hand, "Mimi, can I have one, pleeeeeease?"

Emily smiled and handed her one wrapped in a napkin. She started nibbling on it with a big smile. Emily smiled at Jolene then looked at me. "You know who's going to be most excited about the 'you know what'? You know who…" she said nodding toward Jolene. I took a deep breath. "You're right. I need to tell her in a special way, somehow."

"Didn't you tell me you had robes for each of us the morning of the wedding? Why not put *big sister* on the back?" She whispered.

I broke into a big grin. "Perfect." My phone rang and I saw it was Jay. "Hey, babe," I said winking at his mom.

"Hey, you okay? What did the doctor say?" He sounded so concerned and it made me feel so guilty about keeping it from him.

"I'm going to be fine. It just has to run its course," I said carefully. "I just have to take it easy and I may still have occasional bouts of nausea but he gave me something for that."

"Good, I was worried about you. I know the stress of the wedding has been on your mind and you probably let yourself get worn down." Wow, could he be any more amazing?

"Well, I'm good. Your mom and I were just doing some last minute plans for the wedding and I'll be headed home shortly.   Oh, I wanted to ask you, do you want to go with me to pick up my parents from the airport?" I silently prayed for a yes.

"Sure, I've already met them on Skype so that's out of the way and I know you're probably nervous about seeing them after all that's happened. I'll be there for you, babe," he said.

I shook my head and smiled. "You know I love you more than life itself, right?" I said softly.

"I hope so, because I think I wrote that into the wedding ceremony. That and something about back rubs," he said teasingly.

"I'll promise whatever you promise," I shot back laughing.

"Well, then I'd better get to re-writing my vows. I've got lots to add." Now we were both laughing. "Well, drive safely and I'll see you at home. Give my mom a kiss for me."

"You've got it. She's got a container full of cookies for you, too," I said, taking them from her with a smile.

"Tell her I love her, too," he said before saying goodbye.

I hung up and looked at Emily. "Please tell me I'm doing the right thing by not telling him now."

"You're doing the right thing. Jane, I know you have some trust issues and I think this is the only way to ease them. Let him prove to you what a wonderful man he is and you'll be free from the past and start your marriage on the right foot." She hugged me tightly. "I love you, Jane. I'm so glad my Jay found you and Jolene."

I felt tears welling in my eyes, and I tried in vain to hold back a sob. "You've been so good to us. We're so lucky."

"It's easy to love you both. Now, get out of here and get home. My son's waiting." She walked us to the car and gave us a wave as we drove away.

Chapter 11

Jay

Thursday morning was hectic yet exciting. Jane's parents were flying in and we were all going to meet them at the airport. I knew Jane was nervous about seeing them and I wanted to make things as easy on her as possible. I'd been watching her carefully since she'd had the flu and she seemed to be fine one minute then throwing up the next. She told me it was normal from what the doctor had told her about this particular strain of flu so I made sure she had crackers and ginger ale in the house in case she needed it.

I got up early, got dressed and was ready to take Angel out for her walk when I saw Jolene was already up and dressed with Angel in her harness. "Daddy, Angel was excited to go out, so I got dressed and we're ready to go."

I was so impressed with how helpful she was being and truthfully, Angel had to have been trained at some point because she was very vocal when she needed to go outside. I went back and peeked in on Jane who was still sleeping and Jolene and I took Angel for a walk. I'd made arrangements to get the back yard fenced in so she could be let out but with all the other things going on, we hadn't quite gotten there yet. I also enjoyed my walks with Jolene and Angel because it was daddy/daughter time which was so precious to me. We set off down the street and I held the leash while Jolene held my hand. She was very quiet today and I sensed something was on her mind.

"So, Sweet Pea, what are ya thinking about so hard this morning?" I said lightly.

She glanced up at me and thought for a moment. "I'm scared."

"Scared? What are you scared of?" I said, stopping to look at her.

"I don't know if Grandma and Grandpa will like me. They haven't met me except on the Skype and I want them to like me so they'll keep me," she said with eyes wide.

"Oh, Jolene," I said pulling her in for a hug. "I loved you right away and I know they will too. I'm not leaving you and they won't either."

"Promise, Daddy?" She said hugging me back.

"Yes, ma'am. We're going to be a family." Angel chose that moment to jump up to lick us both in the face. "See, even Angel knows."

Jolene started giggling and I stood up and we continued our walk. "Hey Daddy, what's that sign?" She said pointing to a real estate sign by the sidewalk.

"That means that house is for sale," I answered, stopping to take a look.

"What does that mean?" She asked studying the sign.

"It means that nobody lives there and someone can buy it for their family to live in."

"Can Uncle Justin buy it? I want Ryder to live by me," she said bouncing up and down.

I looked at the house and realized it would be perfect for Justin and Callie. Justin had mentioned looking for something bigger since they had the baby now but he'd really never had the time to look. I took out my phone, snapped a picture of the real estate sign and sent it to Justin. We got back to the house just as Jane was coming out of the bedroom. I could see she was still a wreck about the reunion with her parents. "Have you been sick this morning?" I asked taking the milk out of the fridge to make pancakes for Jolene.

"No, not yet. In fact, I'm really hungry but I don't know what I want," she said digging through the cabinets. "Pop-Tarts. That's what I want."

"You'd rather have that than pancakes?" I said stirring the batter. "You must be sick. Nothing beats my pancakes! Right, Jolene?"

Jolene was sitting with a fork in hand at the table with a big smile on her face. "Yes, Daddy. I love them and I'm staaaarving!"

Jane tore open the foil package and threw her breakfast into the toaster oven. She poured a big glass of milk and put the carton back. I turned around to see her chug the milk like it was a beer at Oktoberfest. She finished drinking, saw my startled expression and looked at me with a sheepish look. "I was thirsty," she mumbled.

"I guess we'll stop and get you some more milk while we're out, then," I said opening the fridge and shaking the nearly empty carton. She just smiled.

I made tiny pancakes so Jolene could manage them by herself and she gobbled them right up. By the time she was finished, Jane was ready to go. We headed to Charlotte/Douglas airport, parked and headed in to wait for Jane's parents' arrival. I held her hand as we walked and could feel the perspiration on her palm. I glanced at her and gave her a smile which she returned with a sickly grin. "Are you feeling bad again?" I asked watching her turn a pale shade of green.

"No, I'll be okay. I'm just nervous," she said taking a deep breath and blowing it back out. "I don't know why I feel this way. They're my mom and dad for God's sake."

I gave her hand a squeeze. "A lot has happened since you saw them last. Just remember, you're not the little teenager they remember. You're a woman with a beautiful daughter and a strikingly good-looking fiancé." I grinned my most goofy grin and got her to laugh. Jolene giggled and I grinned my goofy grin at her as well.

"Daddy, you're so funny!" She said, swinging from my hand as we walked.

Jane was still laughing. "You're such a nut. I love you for making me feel better." She stopped and gave me a quick kiss on the lips. "I'm so glad you're here."

"Well, I had to come and face your dad. I'm sure he's still got an on-sight inspection to do on me," I said laughing.

We found the waiting area near the luggage claim and I watched Jane checking her watch every few minutes. "They should be landing any time now," she said glancing up at the board that announced the arrivals. Jolene was holding tightly to my hand as she watched all the different people walk by.

Suddenly, I felt Jane tense, and I followed her gaze to her parents as they came down the long hallway toward the luggage carousels. I saw her lift her hand to wave and they saw us. Her mom dropped her bag and ran toward us with a huge smile on her face. Jane hesitated then took one step, then another and was soon sprinting toward her mom. When they got to each other, they stopped for a moment then gave each other a tight hug. I felt a tug of emotion watching Jane's face full of happiness and her nervousness was gone in an instant. Her dad who'd stopped to pick up his wife's bag reached them and pulled her in for a tight hug patting her softly on the back. I felt Jolene behind my leg and knew she was back into her shy mode but I wasn't going to force her to meet them until she was comfortable. I saw Jane gesture toward us and smile and I reached down and picked Jolene up to give her a little more security. I walked over and felt Jolene bury her face in my shoulder.

"Jay! It's so nice to finally meet you in person!" Her mom said reaching out to shake my hand since I had my arms full. I shifted Jolene to one arm and grasped her outstretched hand. "You're so handsome and tall. Skype doesn't do you justice," she said smiling.

"It's so nice to meet you too, Mrs. Carter." I reached out my hand to her dad and he gave me a good firm handshake. "Mr. Carter." We had a moment of eye contact and I saw his guard slowly drop and a big smile came over his face.

"Jay, please call me Paul," he insisted. "So the big day's right around the corner. We're so glad we were able to come. Thank you for your generosity."

Jane's mom nodded. "Please call me Sharon. You're going to be family soon." She then started looking around. "So, why didn't you bring Jolene with you today?" She said with a quick wink. I felt Jolene turn her head slightly to peek at Sharon. "I was hoping she'd be here because I was going to give her a special present." Now Jolene was squirming and I knew she was dying to speak but still really shy. She'd drawn a picture for them and was tightly clutching it in her hand behind my back.

"She's going to be here," I said, "but she's just running a little late. She did send you a picture though." She turned, quickly handed Sharon the picture, then hid her face again.

"Oh, this is a beautiful picture! Is this Jolene's new puppy?" She asked looking at the stick-figure Jolene holding a leash attached to a stick figure puppy.

"Yes, you'll get to meet Angel. She's a really good dog and Jolene takes good care of her." I could feel her tension easing and eventually she turned her head to look at them. "You know, I think Jolene could be here any minute now." Jane was standing beside her dad watching with amusement.

I heard Jolene giggle and Sharon looked around in surprise. "Is that her giggling?"

"Could be!" I said slowly relaxing my hold of her. She let me put her down and stood holding my hand.

"Oh my goodness! There she is!" Sharon said kneeling down in front of her. Jolene grinned and put her hand out to shake like she'd seen us do. Sharon took her little hand and shook it. "It's so nice to see you in person! We've brought you a present too."

Paul unzipped the carryon bag he had been holding and pulled out a carefully wrapped package. Jolene's eyes grew big as he handed it to her. "Can I open it?" She asked looking up at Jane and me.

Jane started to laugh but then saw how serious she was. "Of course, baby. It's for you."

"But it's not my birthday or Christmas. This present's wrapped up in paper," she said looking at it with wonder.

"It's fine, baby. That's a special Grandma and Grandpa present and those always come wrapped," Jane assured her. I looked up at Paul and Sharon and saw they were captivated by Jolene. She opened the package and squealed when she saw what was inside. It was a book and she held it up to show Jane, who smiled. "Ah, Rapunzel. Apparently, Grandma and Grandpa must know what you like." She pulled the rest of the paper away to reveal a brand new Rapunzel doll. Jolene just gazed at it in wonder.

"We were hoping you'd like her," Sharon said reaching out to touch the doll.

"I love her!" Jolene said throwing her arms around Sharon's leg. "Thank you Grandma and Grandpa."

There wasn't a dry eye in the group. I cleared my throat. "Well, let's get out of here and get you settled in your hotel," I said heading to the carousel to get their bags.

Paul came with me with their claim tickets and as we stood watching for their bags, he looked at me and smiled. "Thank you for taking such good care of Jane and Jolene. Jane is absolutely glowing and Jolene is obviously in love with her daddy." He looked away as his voice broke. "Tyler did her so wrong and we're so ashamed we waited so long to get in touch with her. We're hopeful we can repair the damage we've done."

I looked at him and patted him on the shoulder. "You're still her parents and she loves you. It'll take time but be patient with her. She's been hurt so much and it's hard for her to give her trust. I know in my heart she loves me but I still doubt she completely trusts me. I'm willing to spend every day of my life proving it to her. I love her and Jolene so much."

Swallowing hard, he nodded. Their bags came around the carousel and we grabbed them and met up with the ladies. Jolene was happily chatting away and I knew she'd overcome her shyness. She had a captive audience and she was working her magic and had them wrapped around her little finger in no time.

We got the Carters settled in their hotel which was near the wedding venue. I'd tried to rent them a car to use while they were visiting but they refused insisting they'd like just to wander around and see the sights on foot. I did insist, however, on getting them a car service for the day of the wedding to take them to the church and reception. They reluctantly agreed and gave me a big hug for all my generosity. I really didn't feel I was being overly generous, they were Jane's family after all. We took them out to a nice dinner at Limone's and then dropped them back off at their hotel. Jane hugged both of them tightly and gave them both a kiss on the cheek. "Thank you for making an effort and being here," she said holding onto their hands.

Sharon's eyes welled up and she could only nod. Paul cleared his throat and suddenly appeared interested in the light fixtures. I knew what they were feeling was genuine and was glad to see it for Jane's sake.

Justin

Callie had a secret and she wasn't sharing. I'd tried to bribe her by promising to change all the poopy diapers for a week but she'd just looked at me like I'd lost my mind. I knew it was something related to Jane but I had no idea what it was. Jay and I were going to the bridal store to pick up our tuxedos and get Paul fitted for his. He was going to be walking Jane down the aisle and the store had picked out a suit close to his measurements to allow for such a quick fitting. After we all got our tuxes situated, we decided to do an impromptu bachelor party at a local pub which consisted of a beer and some pretzels but it was still nice to say we had one. Jane's dad, Paul turned out to be a really nice guy and we sat and talked about baseball and Nascar. Paul was a fan of racing and when I told him the Nascar Hall of Fame was in Charlotte he almost flipped. "We're planning to be here a week, maybe I can convince Sharon to go," he said laughing.

We shot the breeze for a while then headed our separate ways. I got home and saw my little man was relaxing in his baby bouncer. Callie was working on his baby book putting his hospital bracelet and footprint document carefully on the page. She looked up as I walked in. "Hey you. Did you have fun?"

I kissed her on the forehead and knelt down in front of Ryder. "Paul's really nice. I'm glad Jane and her parents are working things out." I scooped Ryder up and gave him a kiss. He was cooing and seemed so content. I sat on the couch and rested him in the crook of my arm.

I watched as Callie worked on his scrapbook. She was so focused and didn't even notice me staring at her. She looked so absolutely beautiful and I felt such a surge of love especially feeling the comforting weight of our child on my arm. This was home. I suddenly remembered the text Jay had sent me earlier of the house in their neighborhood. I pulled out my phone and opened the text. The house was perfect and the location was even better. I knew Callie would be thrilled that it was close to Jane and it would certainly accommodate our growing family. I made a note on my phone to call the real estate agent the next day.

Ryder started making his hungry noises and before I could get up, Callie had automatically stood and gone to the kitchen to warm his bottle. She walked back in, handed it to me and went back to work on her scrapbook. I popped the bottle in his mouth and watched as he gazed at me contentedly. As I watched Callie plans started forming in my head for a special evening we'd been looking forward to since Ryder was born.

The next morning, I called the real estate agent and set up an appointment to see the house. She was going to be in the area, so I made plans to meet her before lunch, and leaving time to get home and get ready for the rehearsal dinner. I pulled up in front of the house and instantly fell in love with it. It was a white two story with a wrapped front porch. I got out of my car and saw the agent was already waiting. "Good morning, Mr. Brisson. I'm Barbara Clarke." She shook my hand and we headed into the house which was vacant. She showed me the beautiful features and several times she mentioned 'move-in ready' and it made me want it even more. By the time I saw the fenced backyard with the fort I was sold.

"I want this house. Whatever they're asking, I'll pay it," I said looking around picturing our family living there.

"Mr. Brisson, I'll give your offer to the owners and I'll get back to you as soon as possible," she said making some notes on her iPad.

I left feeling like I'd won the lottery. I'd thought about how to tell her and devised the perfect plan for the night of our date. I dashed home and found her already dressed and ready to go. Leslie and Tony had volunteered to babysit so this was going to be our first night out since Ryder was born. Callie looked amazing in her sexy black cocktail dress. It hugged her curves which I was now itching to get my hands on. She saw my appraising look and gave me a little hip wiggle which drove me wild. "Seriously? You're going to tempt me like that right before we have to go somewhere?"

She giggled and slowly approached me. I realized she was wearing her stilettos and was eye to eye with me. I watched as she deliberately licked her lips before she purred, "Is it turning you on, Mr. Brisson?" Oh, she had no idea. I wrapped my hands around her waist and pulled her in for a soft sensual kiss. When I let her go she swayed slightly and her eyes were wide. "Wow," was all she could squeak out.

I grinned taking full advantage of my dimples that she loved so much. "Let's go. You're just going to have to wait a little longer," I said with a wink. I heard Leslie and Tony coming up the stairs ready to do their grandparent duty and babysit.

"Are you ready to go?" Leslie asked.

"Yes, Callie's probably gone over all the instructions but if you need anything, please call and we'll come right home," I said opening the door for her.

"Oh, we'll be just fine. Ryder loves his nana and papa," she said heading over to check on him.

"He's just had a bottle so he should be good for a couple of hours," Callie said picking up her purse. "You have all the contact numbers and we'll be home around eleven."

"You kids go have some fun. Don't worry," she said shooing us out the door.

When we were out in the hall we looked at each other and laughed. "I feel like we're forgetting something," Callie said looking at her empty arms. I already miss him."

"I know the feeling but we need this, babe." I took her hand and we headed down to the car.

Chapter 12

Jane

I was getting ready to go to the rehearsal when I felt the nausea hit. "No, not now," I said taking a cool washcloth and dabbing my face. Looking in the mirror I could see how pale and sickly I looked. My mom had mentioned my appearance and was concerned I was coming down with something. Jay explained that I was just recovering from the flu and that seemed to satisfy her but she kept glancing at me during our dinner the night before and watched as I picked at my food. Later that night, I'd been in the bathroom taking my prenatal vitamins when I heard Jay try to open the door. Normally I didn't lock it but I didn't want him to find me choking down a huge pill and ask me what it was for. I wasn't quite ready for the reveal just yet. I'd explained I had just been feeling sickly and didn't want him to walk in to find me huddled over the commode and he seemed to accept that explanation. I only had to get to the wedding tomorrow and give him the special gift bag that I'd put together for him.

Callie and I had gone shopping after work and got some really cute things to put in it. I found a daddy-to-be t-shirt at a local novelty store and a onesie that said 'I Love My Daddy.' I framed the photo of my ultrasound and printed a custom-made 'Father's Day' card. It read, "See you next year!" The bag itself looked like a tuxedo and totally fit the wedding theme. He wouldn't suspect a thing. My plan was to have Justin take the bag to him while they were getting ready.

I leaned against the sink feeling the nausea pass and with a touch-up of my makeup, I went to join Jay. He looked so handsome in his suit and was looking at me with such love and it made my heart beat faster knowing that I was carrying this beautiful man's child. "I've dropped off Jolene at Maegan's. She was thrilled to watch her for the night and was even more excited to be coming to the wedding tomorrow." He took me by the hand and lifted it to his lips placing a gentle kiss on my skin. I felt shivers as he gazed at me. "I love you so much and can't wait to marry you tomorrow."

I couldn't speak for a moment. I just looked into his deep green eyes and brushed the hair away from his eyes. "I love you too."

We walked hand in hand to the car and drove to the rehearsal dinner still keeping our hands touching. As we arrived at the restaurant, we saw my parents walking up and they gave us warm hugs before we walked inside to greet our family and friends. I saw Callie already seated and Justin was pulling out Emily's chair for her at the table we'd had reserved for us. We joined them and Jay made sure to pull my chair out for me brushing my arm with his hand and I felt tingles where he'd touched. Jay stood beside me and greeted everyone. As the buzz of voices quieted, he held up a glass of wine and said, "Welcome friends and family. Jane and I are so blessed to have you with us for this wonderful occasion." Everyone lifted their glass as well and reluctantly I did too. I was afraid to drink so when everyone clinked glasses, I joined in and quickly pretended to sip some wine. Callie and Emily were watching me and I felt my face flush. Jay sat down and put his hand on my thigh absently stroking my skin with his thumb. I was on fire. It seemed that every touch, every look was making me want him so badly and I wondered if it was related to my hormones. "You okay, babe?" Jay asked looking at me.

"Sure, why?" I answered, looking at him with confusion.

"Well, I could've sworn you said, 'Not hormones.' What were you talking about?"

I'd apparently spoken out loud. "No, I said this is like Limone's. The wine, it tastes like the wine at Limone's."

Callie was taking a drink of her wine as I answered and almost spit it across the table. Justin looked over and put his hand on her back. "Are you okay, Cal?" He asked rubbing her gently.

"Yes, I'm just fine," she said laughing. "Can't take me anywhere, can you?"

Everyone at the table started laughing and thankfully the attention was off of me. We'd decided in lieu of a traditional rehearsal, since we had such a small wedding party, we would just do a verbal walk-through. My dad was thrilled to be escorting me down the aisle and I was really emotional thinking of how I'd feel when they opened the doors and I could see Jay waiting for me. Or at least I hoped so.

Our dinners arrived and we ate with just the occasional small talk. My parents were describing Portland to everyone and they were fascinated. My dad invited everyone out to visit and we all promised that eventually we'd have to make a trip. The evening ended and I was reaching for my purse when I felt Callie grab my arm. "Are you okay? All night long you looked like you wanted to throw Jay down on the table and have your way with him!"

"What?! I did not!" I stammered.

"You've got to be kidding me," she scoffed. "You watched his every move and I swear if you licked your lips once, you licked them a hundred times."

"I have dry lips!" I countered.

"Yeah, okay. You can't lie to me," she said laughing. "Are you going to sleep together tonight or are you going with the traditional sleeping apart thing?"

I finally couldn't keep up the façade. "I can't stop thinking about him! I'm so freaking turned on right now I could probably lure him into a dark corner and have my way with him. I don't remember feeling this way when I was pregnant with Jolene."

She laughed out loud. "Well, first of all, you weren't with a man and if you'd acted like that around me, I would've sprayed you with cold water!" I laughed as she continued. "Secondly, I doubt it's hormones because I felt no attraction at all to Justin for the first trimester but after that, it was all I could think about. I think you just love the man so much and can't wait to be his bride."

I looked over at Jay who was standing with my dad and felt a rush of need and lust and nodded. "I really hope he doesn't run, Callie. I don't think I could handle it."

"He'll be there. I put the bag in Justin's car, made him pinky swear not to look in it and told him to deliver it to Jay the minute he gets to the church," she said patting me on the shoulder.

"God, I hope so," I sighed.

Jay came over and put his arm around me. "I'm going to steal my fiancée away for the night. She needs her rest so she can dance down the aisle to marry me tomorrow," he said before placing a gentle kiss on my forehead.

"She's all yours," Callie said squeezing my hand.

We drove back to the house and as we walked in, I saw an overnight bag by the door. I stopped still and stared at it. Jay walked over and picked it up. "I'm going to stay at my mom's tonight. I hear it's a traditional thing and I want this to be perfect. You'll have the whole bed to yourself and tomorrow Callie and my mom will pick you up to get ready at the church."

"You're leaving?" I asked my voice breaking.

"Not leaving, just spending the last night of my bachelorhood with my mom. I'll see you tomorrow at the church." He leaned over and kissed me softly on the lips. "I love you, Jane." I closed my eyes to keep the tears from falling down my cheeks and I heard the door open and close and he was gone. I went into the bedroom and threw myself down on the bed. I couldn't keep the tears in check and just sobbed until I couldn't cry anymore. Eventually, exhausted I fell asleep.

The doorbell woke me the next morning and I heard Callie yelling for me to open the door. I crawled off the bed and suddenly realized I was still in my clothes from the night before. I quickly stripped off my dress and threw on my robe. As I opened the door, Callie was in mid-knock and almost rapped me on the nose.

"Wow, what happened to you last night?" She said walking in looking around for signs of some crazy party that would explain my disheveled appearance and mascara streaked face.

"Jay left," I sighed. She stopped and stared at me. "Well, not left but went to his mom's. He said it was the traditional thing to do."

"Oh, so you didn't get to jump his bod when you got home and instead chose to cry yourself to sleep?" She said walking into the kitchen to put some coffee on.

I threw myself down in the kitchen chair. "Pretty much," I mumbled. "Why am I letting this ruin what should be one of the best days of my life?"

"Jane, you've had a pretty sucky hand dealt to you so far and Jay's your Powerball winning ticket," she said rummaging in the cupboard for cups.

"Did you buy a Powerball ticket on the way over?" I said studying her.

"Well, if you must know, yes. I guess that's where the gambling metaphors are coming from," she said laughing. "The jackpot's amazing right now and that's the only time I try to win."

I sighed. "You're right. I guess the gift bag will be delivered and my fate is set. No use in ruining the day."

"That's the spirit, now throw yourself in the shower and let's get a move on. The hair and makeup people will be at the church in an hour." She handed me a cup of coffee and shooed me out of the kitchen.

I drank some coffee and felt better. I got in the shower and let the water run over my head trying to wash away the doubt and worry and after a while I felt the water starting to cool off and realized I'd better get out and get in gear.

I threw on my sweats and blew my hair dry leaving it unstyled so they could fix it when I got to the church. When I came back into the kitchen I saw Emily had arrived and was having a cup of coffee with Callie. They were actually discussing me when I came in.

"I almost choked when she had to pretend-sip her wine," Emily was saying.

Callie was laughing. "I lost it when she said 'not hormones' sounded like not like Limone's."

"All right, enough, I'm right here," I said standing at the kitchen door with my hand on my hip.

"Shhhh…she's here," Callie whispered loudly.

Emily stood to give me a hug. "Jay didn't sleep well if it's any consolation. He was up late working on his vows but I'm not supposed to tell you that."

"He lied to me!" I said with surprise. "He told me he wrote those weeks ago."

"I didn't say he was writing them, he was working on them. Big difference," Emily said laughing.

"Oh, well, you're right. That does make a difference," I conceded.

We gathered our things, most importantly my dress, and packed everything in the limo which had now arrived to take us to the church. I could feel the nerves building as we pulled up at the side entrance and I saw Maegan and her husband Nate surrounded by their beautiful little girls in a variety of brightly colored dresses. Jolene was holding her hand and ran over to the car when we were getting out. "Mama! Did you bring my dress?"

"Yes, sweetie, I did." We'd picked out a beautiful dress that was bright pink with a navy sash and a band of navy around the bottom of the knee-length skirt. I gave Maegan a hug and thanked her so much for taking care of Jolene for the night.

"Girl, it was no problem! Those kids get along like a house on fire. They know if they misbehave that I'll get my flip flop after them," she said laughing.

"Well, you've been such a great friend and after we get back from our honeymoon, we plan to have a big barbeque and have you over," I said giving her another hug.

"Barbeque?" Nate said looking around. "Did somebody say barbeque?"

"Another day, Nate," I said laughing. "Tonight you'll have to suffer through steak or chicken."

"Well, a guy's gotta do what a guy's gotta do. I guess I can suffer through," he said shaking his head while giving me a wink.

I heard a throat clear behind me and saw Callie tapping her foot. "Woman, we've got to get you ready."

"Sorry," I said to Callie before waving at Maegan, Nate and their brood.

We got into the church dressing room and I saw everything was set up to beautify us. A rack was against the wall with our robes on hangers and our names were neatly printed on it so we could find the right one. Jolene's was pretty obvious since it was the smallest but hers also had a special designation on the back. I didn't say a word as I helped her put it on. I was going to wait until we were all finished with our primping. I slipped my robe on and sat in the chair while my mom and Emily put theirs on and let the hairstylists do their thing. Both having short hair, theirs didn't take long but the results were amazing. They moved to the makeup chairs while Callie and I took our turn with the hairstylists. My stylist was Josie and she did my hair in an updo with a cascade of ringlets falling softly in the back. She placed the tiara and I heard my mom gasp. "Jane, you look like a princess!" Jolene, who had been watching the whole process nodded with her mouth slightly open.

I looked in the mirror and had to admit, I did look like a princess. I was getting ready to go to the makeup chair when we heard a knock at the door.

"Yes?" Callie called out.

"It's me, Jay." My heart skipped a beat. "I need to see Jane right now."

He sounded upset and I closed my eyes squeezing back the tears that threatened to come.

"It's bad luck to see the bride, Jay," Emily said with a smile.

"Let me in, now!"

Eyes wide, Emily opened the door. Jay's eyes locked on mine and never wavered as he walked in. "Could you give us some privacy?" He said still focused on me.

Everyone scattered and within moments we were all alone. I began, "Jay, I—"

He moved so quickly I didn't have time to register what was happening but the next thing I knew I was in his arms and his mouth was crushing mine in a searing kiss. I felt my body go lax in his arms and my knees threatened to buckle. His hands spanned my back as he pulled me closer until our bodies were pressed tightly together. Finally, he slowed the kiss ending it with a gentle peck.

"I got my gift bag," he said with a smile.

"And?" I managed to whisper.

"And I'm the luckiest man on earth. I'm so happy that we're having a baby together. It's what I've always wanted to share with you. I had to come and tell you because in my heart I knew you were worried that I'd run. Well, the only place I want to be is here with you. Plus," he said reaching in his pocket, "I had to bring you my present too." I looked down and saw a tiny box. I took it from him and opened it to find a perfect solitaire diamond suspended from a delicate chain. He reached into the box, lifted it out and draped it around my neck. As he fastened it, he kissed the bare nape of my neck then softly growled. "I've just got one thing to say... you'd better get your makeup on and get out there because you're wasting precious time. I want you to be mine and it's killing me to have to wait," he said cupping my face.

"I'll be right there," I whispered as I spun around to drape my arms around his neck then slowly licked my lips before pressing them to his.

"Whoa, we'd better get this wedding going soon. I want to hurry up and get to the honeymoon," he said taking a towel from the table and dabbing his forehead.

"Still won't tell me where we're going?" I asked pouting.

"Nope, you'll find out when we get to the airport," he laughed. "Oops, I said airport…now you'll figure it out."

"Jay, you are such a nut. Get out of here and let us get dressed. I'll see you in a few." I pushed him toward the door. "Oh, and one more thing, I love you."

He grinned and gave me a wink. "Of course you do, I'm a catch!"

We opened the door and Callie, Jane and my mom came tumbling in. The only one who hadn't been eavesdropping was Jolene who was happily spinning in the hallway with her robe flaring. She stopped when she saw Jay and I standing there. "Jay, could you tell Jolene what her robe says?" I said giving him a wink.

He spun her around and knelt down behind her. "Hmm, it says BIG SISTER!"

Jolene turned around and looked at the both of us with wide eyes. "BIG SISTER? Why do I have that on my back?"

I rubbed my tummy and smiled. "Because we're having a baby."

Jolene's squeal pierced the air. "A BABY! I'm gonna have a baby brother?"

"Or a sister," I finished for her.

"YAY!" She said jumping up and down.

My mom who had been standing over to the side and hadn't noticed Jolene's robe before had tears in her eyes. "Baby, I'm so happy for you both. I promise we'll be here for you this time. We missed out on so much with Jolene but we promise to make that up to you and the new baby."

"Thanks, Mom," I said with tears welling up.

Jay stood and hugged me one last time. "I'm ready to get married. You people do what you need to do to get my bride ready as soon as possible. I'll be waiting in the front of the church, center aisle."

The hairstylist worked on Jolene while we were getting our makeup done. Jolene's hair was pulled back leaving her curls cascading down her back and I'd gotten a bright pink headband with a huge pink flower on it.

We slipped her into her dress and marveled at how grown up she looked. Callie made sure everyone was perfect and when we got the knock that they were ready for the mothers, I had just slipped on my dress. Before she left, my mom handed me a delicate ring with a cameo on it. "This was my mother's so this is your something old." She slipped it on my right ring finger and I could feel tears prickling my eyelids so I blew out a deep breath to stop myself from breaking down. I hugged her and whispered, "I love you, Mom."

Emily stepped up next. "Jane, I'm so glad Jay found you and I'm so happy I'm going to be a grandmother to both of your children. This is your something blue." I looked down as she wrapped a delicate chain around my wrist and suspended from it was a deep blue sapphire. I blew out my breath again as I hugged her tightly.

"Thank you for everything, including Jay." Emily smiled and then she and my mom headed out to the vestibule to be seated leaving Callie, Jolene and me.

"Wow," Callie said. "That was pretty intense, huh?" I could only nod still trying to fight back the tears. "Well, let's see. You've got the old, the new thanks to Jay, and the blue. That means you need something borrowed. I think I'll have to take care of that. She reached up and slipped the stud earrings out of my ears. "Technically, Justin bought these for me," she began, "but when I really looked at them, I decided they'd look amazing on you today so you are 'borrowing' my new earrings." She put the earrings on my ears and turned me to the mirror. They were diamond drop earrings and they looked perfect with my necklace. "Oh and in case you're wondering, he went to Jared," she said laughing.

I wanted to cry but I ended up laughing and hugging my best friend as tightly as I could. "I love you," I simply said.

"And I you," she countered.

We heard a knock at the door and heard, "It's time."

Jolene grabbed her flower basket which was embellished with a big pink ribbon and smiled. "Mama, I'm not going to dump them out this time."

I laughed remembering Callie's wedding and how small she'd really been. The difference in her was amazing. As she'd walked down the aisle at Callie's wedding she'd dumped the entire contents of the basket on the floor as she entered the door. This time, we'd explained how she could take a handful at a time and make them last all the way down. She loved that idea especially since Jay was going to be waiting at the head of the church for her.

We walked out into the vestibule and I saw my dad standing by the door. He looked at me and I saw him swallow hard and knew he was feeling a lot of emotions about today. I was too and I found myself blowing out little puffs of air again to keep from crying.

Jolene stood at the open doors and as the music started she slowly stepped down the aisle. I wasn't allowed in front of the door so I missed her walk the entire way but I saw the first handful and she did it perfectly. I heard her voice ring out in the church as she continued down the aisle, "I'm gonna be a big sister!" I heard a smatter of applause and a whoo! Callie grinned, stepped up to the door, and gave me a thumbs up before turning and stepping down the aisle. The director of the wedding then shut the huge doors and we heard the music continue for a few moments before it stopped and became the wedding march. The director placed my dad and me in front of the doors then she dramatically threw them open. All I could see was Jay's face when he saw me. His eyes lit up and he had the biggest smile on his face. I didn't see anyone else but Jay as I walked slowly up the aisle with my dad. I felt my fingers gripping his arm and he placed his hand on top of mine to calm me. It wasn't nerves that were causing me to clutch onto my dad, it was the emotional overload that washed over me when I saw Jay and knew this was it.

We reached Jay and he put out his hand for me to hold on to. The minister asked, "Who gives this woman to be wed?" and my father replied in a strong voice, "Her mother and I."

He stepped away to sit with my mom and I felt Jay's thumb softly stroking my skin and it soothed my trembling hand. I handed Callie my bouquet as the minister began the ceremony and I remember him speaking about joining our lives together to create a family. Jolene was standing beside me watching us with a huge smile on her face.

I heard the minister ask Jay to recite his vows. Jay turned to me and held both of my hands. "Jane, in your eyes, I've found my home. In your heart, I've found my love. In your soul, I've found my mate. You've given me a lifetime of happiness already and it can only get better as we move forward to the future. You make me laugh and I hurt when you cry. You're my breath, my every heartbeat. I'm yours and you're mine. You'll own my heart, forever." He slipped my ring onto my finger.

I stood there looking at this amazing man who had now taken my breath away with his beautiful words. I swallowed hard and tried to keep my voice from breaking as I recited mine to him. "Jay, you're my inspiration and my heart's desire. You bring magic to my life and you've shown me a love I'd never thought possible. You make me feel safe and I trust you with my life. You've shown me every day how truly amazing you are and I thank God that you're mine. You'll always have my undying love." I slipped his ring onto his finger.

The minister then said that Jay had something special to say to Jolene. Wide-eyed, she walked up to stand between us. "Jolene, I wasn't there when you took your first steps but I'll be with you now every step of your life from this day forward. I love you, Sweet Pea." He reached in his pocket and pulled out a ring box which he cracked open to reveal a tiny ring with Jolene's birthstone in it. He plucked the ring from the box and taking her hand, slid it onto her finger. She smiled as she looked up at him. "Thank you, Daddy."

We all held hands as the minister pronounced, "Ladies and gentlemen, I'd like to introduce the Anderson family."

Our family and friends erupted in applause and we gave each other a kiss and then both bent down to give Jolene one on each cheek. We all walked down the aisle together then waited for the guests to come out to give their congratulations.

****

Jay

I was sitting in the pew watching the photographer arranging Jane and her parents for their family photo and my mind wandered back to this morning when I'd arrived at the church. Justin was already there and he met me at the door to the men's dressing area. "Hey, Jay. How're you feeling? Nervous?"

I looked at him and felt surprisingly calm. "No, not a bit. Were you on your wedding day?"

"No, but I thought it was a fluke. I'm glad I'm not the only one. It must mean we're doing the right thing," he said slapping me on the back.

We started unpacking our tuxedos and he stopped and looked at me with a funny expression. "I'll be right back," he said before dashing out the door. He returned a couple of minutes later carrying a gift bag that looked like a tuxedo. "Callie and Jane would've killed me if I'd forgotten to give you this." He handed the bag to me and continued unpacking his tux.

I'd walked over to a table and set the bag down. I'd reached in and pulled out the card. Opening it and saw it was a homemade Father's Day card and it made me smile. Obviously Jolene had wanted me to have something special and even though it wasn't Father's Day the sentiment was appreciated. I'd opened the card and read 'See you next year' but no name signed. Puzzled, I reached in the bag and pulled out a t-shirt that was rolled up. I laid it on the table and slowly unrolled it to reveal a baby's onesie tucked inside. The onesie read 'I love my Daddy' and the shirt read 'Daddy to-be'. I couldn't figure out why Jane had gotten me the onesie because obviously it was for a baby so I reached in the bag and pulled out the last item which was a photograph in a frame. I stared at it and it all fell into place. Justin came up behind me and slapped me on the back again. "Looks like someone's gonna be a dad," he said laughing. I looked up to see Jane's father standing there with a shocked expression on his face but within a few moments, he broke into a huge grin.

"Are you serious?" He said walking over to stand beside me. "Congratulations, Jay."

"I've got to see Jane…now," I said grabbing my gift box for her and dashing out of the room. As I jogged to the room where the girls were getting ready I slowed and then finally stopped. I had to think. She wanted me to know before the wedding for a reason. She could've told me when we were together but instead chose to do it while we were apart. Suddenly, it hit me. This was a test. She was giving me an out and was probably a ball of knots waiting until she walked into the church where she'd find me waiting. Or not. I caught my breath and slowly made my way to the dressing room. I'd decided not to give anything away until we were completely alone. When I knocked and asked to see Jane I got the resistance I'd expected but when I insisted, the door opened and I saw Jane and no one else. As everyone scattered and we were left alone, I knew the only way to prove to her how I felt was to give her the kiss of a lifetime and when I felt her melt into my arms, I knew I'd finally broken through.

My daydreaming was interrupted by the photographer asking me to join the family shot. Standing beside my wife with her parents on one side, my mom on the other, and Jolene in front of us, I realized how beautiful this moment was. The photographer was winding down the pictures and it was time for the pictures of just the two of us. We posed holding hands and recreated the kiss and then I had a special request. I turned Jane's back to me and placed my hand on her still flat tummy. She glanced back over her shoulder at me and placed her hand on top of mine. I then asked Jolene to come and stand beside me and hold my hand. The photographer looked at us and smiled. "I'm guessing, but I'd say congratulations are in order." He snapped the picture and we had our first family portrait together.

We headed over to the reception and thankfully they'd started serving some food to keep the crowd happy. I heard the DJ announce our arrival and then it was time for our first dance as a couple. I'd chosen a song that had special meaning and as the first notes started, I saw Jane's eyes light up with recognition. "This is the song we danced to at Callie and Justin's wedding!" She said as I pulled her close and I heard her sigh as she laid her head on my shoulder. We swayed to 'I Won't Give Up' by Jason Mraz just like we'd done that very special night. It was the night I'd finally had the courage to tell her how I felt and that I wanted to be with her. This time when we danced, she was my wife and I knew I'd never have to worry about not having her in my life ever again. I whispered in her ear, "I love you, Mrs. Anderson." She lifted her head and smiled as I kissed her softly on the forehead. The song ended and I heard the DJ ask for the father/daughter dance. Paul came over and put out his hand for Jane and I went in search of Jolene. She was sitting at the kiddie table with the triplets and I walked up and held out my hand. "I believe it's my turn to ask you, Sweet Pea." She looked at me and grinned.

"Daddy, is this our dance?" She said jumping up to grasp my hand.

"It sure is," I replied leading her out to the dance floor. Jane was watching us as the music started and I heard Heartland's song 'I Loved Her First'. My heart skipped a beat as I realized how emotional this song was and I was now dancing with my daughter. Jolene had grown taller since the last time we'd danced and she didn't need to stand on my shoes this time. She held my hands and swayed back and forth and smiled. I looked over at Jane who'd had to steal her dad's hankie to dab her eyes and winked. She smiled back at me and I felt so at peace. This was my family and I was so blessed.

We partied until most of the crowd had thinned out and finally it was time to head off to our honeymoon. We changed out of our wedding attire and started saying our goodbyes. Jolene was going to be staying with my mom and Jane's parents had asked to spend time with her while we were gone which we agreed to but only with my mom present. Despite the reconciliation, Jane still felt Jolene didn't know them that well and it would be good for them to get to know each other through short visits. We hugged everyone and I had to promise to bring Jolene a present from our trip but I was still vague and wouldn't say where we were going. She gave us big wet kisses and waved goodbye as we drove away in the limo.

Our car arrived at the airport and Jane was trying to figure out where we were headed. I knew I couldn't keep it from her forever but I'd managed to arrange for us to be presented with leis as we entered the first class lounge. Her eyes grew wide. "We're going to Hawaii?" She squealed.

"Yes and it's a long flight so you'll have plenty of time to rest before we get there," I said pulling her to me for a kiss. "You're gonna need all the rest you can get for this honeymoon."

"You're too much, Mr. Anderson. First class to Hawaii? I think I've hit the jackpot with you," she giggled.

"No babe, it's me who's won the jackpot," I said hugging her tightly. We sat in the lounge and when the flight was called we boarded and after a quick stop in Atlanta, we arrived in Honolulu twelve hours later.

Jane slept most of the flight and I occupied myself with cat naps and movies. When we got off the plane, we were greeted with fresh leis and a driver was waiting to take us to our condo. I'd spared no expense wanting to make this trip one to remember. I'd booked us into the Aston Waikiki Beach Tower and we had a two-bedroom suite to be able to stretch out and enjoy ourselves. Once we'd gotten settled in our room, Jane wandered out onto the lanai to take in the view.

"Isn't it breathtaking?" She called back to me.

I came up behind her slipping my hands around her waist. "The only sight that takes my breath away is you," I said nuzzling her neck. She turned in my arms to face me and threw her arms around my neck.

"All of my dreams have come true and it's all because of you," she said softly.

I touched my forehead to hers. "I can say the exact same thing about you, babe."

She leaned back to look into my eyes. "They say you shouldn't hope for the fairytale but I've definitely found my prince."

I softly kissed her lips and backed her toward our king-sized bed. "I think it's time to show you how much I've wanted you, princess."

"I'm intrigued…Mr. Anderson," she purred.

"Do you know how hot you make me when you say that?" I groaned as we tumbled onto the bed.

"I think I'm getting ready to find out," she said smiling up at me.

"How did I get so lucky? You're the most beautiful woman in the world and you're all mine. I can't even wrap my mind around that," I said before softly nuzzling her neck. She moaned and turned her head slightly to offer more of her velvety smooth skin. As I feathered kisses down her neck to her shoulder, I slowly unbuttoned her white cotton shirt to expose her lacy bra. I slid my fingers under the strap and pulled it down to expose more of that delicious skin. Her hand, which had been lying still on my shoulder slowly slid up to tangle in my hair. I could feel her breath quickening and the pulse in her neck was racing. She gazed at me with hooded eyes and she lightly pushed me until I was on my back.

Scooting up onto her knees, she straddled me. Her hair was hanging over her face as she finished unbuttoning her shirt which she now removed completely. She swung her shirt like a lasso flinging it where it landed on top of a lamp. My eyes widened as I saw a hunger in her eyes. "I've wanted you so badly and now I've got you where I want you." She leaned down and nipped my earlobe as her hands unbuttoned my shirt and then her hands roamed my bare chest. She was wearing shorts, her bare legs were now touching my body and I took advantage of having access to those long beautiful legs. Trailing my fingers from her ankles up to her hips I saw her shiver with excitement. She slanted her mouth over mine and kissed me, her breath coming now in quick pants. My hands now slid up her back to find the clasp of that sexy bra and within seconds, I had it unclasped and was free to run my hands over her bare back. She purred as I softly massaged her warm skin. She sat up and never taking her eyes off mine, she unbuttoned my shorts. After unzipping them, she slid her body down my legs tugging my shorts along with her. My shorts followed the path of her shirt. She crawled back up the bed like a puma and for a moment I thought I heard her growl. "Babe?" I whispered. "Please be gentle with me."

She threw back her head and chuckled. "I guess I am being a little aggressive, huh?" She said unbuttoning her shorts. "I thought it was hormonal but I think it's just that you're smokin' hot and you're all mine for the taking."

I threw my arms out onto the bed and laid my head back on the pillow. "Then have your way with me, woman," I said surrendering to her.

A few moments later, the rest of our clothes were tossed aside and my hands were exploring her beautiful curves. Her face was flushed, her lips red and moist from our kisses. She looked more beautiful than I thought possible. I never thought I could love someone so much. Our limbs tangled, we caressed each other, unhurried in our lovemaking knowing that we had the rest of our lives to share this beautiful experience. Our passion intensified and we found ourselves holding each other tightly. The sensations were overwhelming, the emotions so raw and real that I knew Jane had finally let go of her past and given herself completely to me. Instead of crying out my name, she softly whispered, "I love you." I kissed her softly and held her allowing her to fall exhausted in the bed. I pulled her close to me, resting my hand on her waist. She slid her hand on top of mine and we fell asleep cradling our child.

Chapter 13

Justin

Jay and Jane had come back from their honeymoon tanned and relaxed and although I was happy for them, I was also jealous that they'd had quality time together. Having Ryder was the best thing that had ever happened to us but it also had put a serious crimp in our love life. I'd been secretly counting down the days until Callie's six week checkup and had been formulating a plan to get her alone without interruptions. I enlisted the aid of Leslie and Tony who were more than willing to babysit overnight, the only problem was Callie. She was so attached to Ryder that she'd not left him since the night of the rehearsal dinner. My parents had held Ryder during the wedding which he slept through, thank God but after that she'd been with him 24/7. I'd stayed busy negotiating with the real estate people behind her back and had bought the house near Jay and Jane without her knowing. My plan was to blindfold her revealing our new home when we arrived. Jane was excited about our moving so close to them but I made her swear not to tell Callie and she reluctantly agreed. I scheduled everything with Leslie and the plan was to have them just show up and then I would essentially kidnap her for the night.

The big day finally arrived and I waited all afternoon for the verdict. I was with an important client when my phone vibrated with a text. It was Callie.

It's all good ;)

I had a hard time concentrating after that but I managed to get through the meeting and immediately called Leslie. "So, are you interested in watching Ryder this weekend?" I asked trying to keep the pleading tone to a minimum.

"Oh, sure! We'd love to!" She said laughing. "Justin, you're so transparent I can see right through you!"

"It's that obvious?" I groaned. "I miss my wife."

"I know, sweetie. Believe me, she's probably feeling that way too right about now. You need that time after the baby comes to adjust and she wasn't in that place for a while." I couldn't believe I was talking about my love life with my mother-in-law. "She's feeling better about herself and she's getting some sleep. You both deserve some time alone to reconnect."

If she'd been standing in front of me I would have kissed her! "Thank you for understanding and being such a great mom and nana."

"Justin, I'm so proud of the both of you and love you so much. I've already bought Ryder some goodies for this weekend too. Never too soon to start spoiling him. By the way, Tony and I have been buying him stocks. He has a portfolio!"

I started laughing. "Why am I picturing Ryder on tv talking about trading stocks?

She joined in on the laughter. "Oh, I love those commercials!"

"Well, my plan for this weekend is simple. Take her out of town to Charlotte, back to the hotel where we first met, so I'll give you all the information in case you need us."

"We'll be fine, Justin. I did a pretty good job raising Callie. I might be a bit scattered sometimes but when it comes to my grandson, I'm giving one hundred percent."

"See you tomorrow, about noon?" I asked as I grabbed my briefcase before heading out the door to go home.

"We'll be there!" She said cheerily.

I stopped on the way home and grabbed a few things to take with us for the weekend. The clerk at the store was very helpful and within a few minutes, I had everything I needed to make this weekend perfect. I left everything in the car except for the blindfold which I tucked in my pants pocket.

I walked into the condo and the first thing I noticed was the aroma of something delicious. I set my briefcase down and eased up behind her slipping my hands around her waist. She had her hair up in a clip which gave me easy access to that part of her neck I loved to bite and as I lightly nipped her skin, I saw her shiver. "What's the special occasion that we get homemade Chicken Lo Mein?"

"You'd better stop that Justin or you won't get any Lo Mein at all," she said giggling. "You just might get lucky."

I had to think quickly because I wanted to wait until tomorrow night when we could be focused on each other not the baby monitor. I yawned, "Callie, I had a long day today. We may just have to postpone that another day or so. Let me build up my strength."

She pursed her lips then went with an all-out pout. "You mean to tell me that you've waited all this time and you're tired? You knew this day was coming, you should have been resting more."

I laughed. "You make it sound like a marathon."

Her brows raised as she looked around at me. "It is…at least that's what I've been counting on."

"Well, baby, we can wait a few more days. I'm just worn out. I don't get to lie around all day at home." I knew I'd probably make her mad with the last line but I needed her out of the mood, at least for the time being.

"LAY AROUND? Is that what you think I do all day? Justin Allen Brisson, you have no idea what I do," she said angrily throwing the chicken in with the noodles.

"Callie, calm down, you're abusing my noodles. I didn't mean you don't do anything. I know you take care of the baby but I'm out making multi-million dollar projects come to life and you've been out of the game for a while now. I'm tired."

She threw back her head and sighed. "You're right. You do go to work and I'm ready to go back myself. I just can't break away from Ryder. I love him so much and I'm afraid if I go to work, he'll do something amazing and I'll have to hear about it from some daycare or babysitter." She wiped her eyes with the back of her hand. "I just want life to be normal again. I miss my job and yet I'd miss him more."

I turned her around in my arms and pressed her against the counter. "You don't have to go back to the office. Jay and Jane are doing fine with you doing work from home and with the internet such a big part of what we do, you can still design and be a part of that world but still be here for Ryder."

Her eyes were lowered and I placed my hand under her chin to make her look at me. "I love you and your place is wherever you feel it needs to be. Don't work for my sake and don't stay home for it either."

She started to say something and we heard the sound of Ryder waking up on the monitor. "I'd better go check him," she said turning off the stove.

"I'll go so you can finish what you're doing. I've missed my little man today," I said heading to the nursery. As I walked in, I could see Ryder kicking his legs and swinging his fists while he made cooing noises and as I got closer, the kicking kicked into high gear.

"How's daddy's little man?" I said leaning over the crib. His eyes followed me as I walked over to get a diaper and he got excited as I picked him up to put him on his changing table. I unfastened his diaper and the most amazingly horrible smell hit me. "Dude, what have you been eating?" I managed to choke out.

He just gazed at me and wiggled his hands. I pulled the diaper down and saw he'd left a nice present for me and as I reached to get the wipes ready, he put his foot right down in it. "No! Gosh what a mess!" As fast as I was with a wipe, the faster he was with his feet. He ended up getting dirtier than the diaper when we were through. I pulled the offending diaper away and dumped it in the Diaper Genie wishing I had an air freshener around my neck to ease my discomfort. "I swear I don't know how that much stuff can come out of such a little guy." He just looked up at me with those big blue eyes and I laughed. "You can't help it, can you, buddy?" I finished putting his new diaper on and was just snapping his onesie when I heard a noise and turned around to see Callie standing there with the monitor from the other room.

"I could hear everything you said, Justin…DUDE? You're teaching our son the word DUDE?"

I shrugged my shoulders. "He may end up with a career in surfing and he'll be all set." I scooped him up and carried him cradled to my shoulder out of the room. "Ryder said he's hungry and so is his daddy." She followed behind me with a puzzled look but I just pretended not to see it. She got Ryder a bottle and got him fed while I got the plates out and dished out the food. I ate slowly and I could see she was getting irritated but I had to make this plan work and tonight wasn't the night for romance.

After dinner, I took the baby and sat holding him for a while watching her out of the corner of my eye getting frustrated. At about nine, I put Ryder to bed and yawned loudly. "Well, I'm going to get to bed. I've got some errands to run tomorrow morning and I need my sleep." I saw her face fall and I hated hurting her but she had no idea how wonderful her weekend was going to be.

I went to bed and I heard her come in and sigh loudly but I pretended to be asleep. She stood looking down at me for a while then went to get ready for bed. I felt her crawl into bed and she turned her back to me which made me feel bad so I rolled over and threw my arm around her as if dreaming. She sighed again and eventually we both fell asleep.

She had to get up with the baby a couple of times during the night and I heard her get up but didn't move. When first light came, I got up, gave Ryder his bottle and put him back to bed. I grabbed my running clothes, threw them on and dashed out before she woke up. I got a text from her when she woke up asking where I was and I couldn't tell her. My errand story wasn't a lie. I needed to finish getting my goodies for our date. I stopped at the jewelers to pick up the gift I'd ordered earlier in the week and then stopped by the hardware store. I made a quick stop at the florist and then into the local spa to pick up a gift card.

Leslie called about eleven and said they were getting ready to come over. I got home and literally looked like I'd been working out because I was sweating from hustling around. Callie looked at me as I came in but then quickly looked away. I jogged into the bathroom and took a quick shower making sure to grab my overnight bag which I tucked behind the door of the closet.

I was coming out of the closet when I almost ran right into her. She had a hurt look and I stopped when I saw tears welling in her eyes. "Justin, is there something you're not telling me?" She was holding her hand behind her back.

"Excuse me? What are you talking about?" I asked puzzled.

"This," she said bringing her hand around and that's when I saw it. The blindfold. She must have found it in my pocket when she was doing the laundry. "Can you explain this?" The look on her face was so tortured and I knew what she was thinking. I'd come home worn out and tired because I'd been out playing fifty shades with some hoochie.

"Callie, I can explain," I began. "It's not what you think." I was interrupted by the doorbell and I saw her shake her head with frustration. "Let me get that and then we'll straighten this out, okay?" I said heading for the door.

I opened the door and was relieved to see it was Leslie and Tony. Callie looked confused as her mom breezed in with arms full of bags. Tony carried an overnight bag in with him and as he set it down and hugged her she finally found her voice. "What's going on?" She stammered. "Are you moving in?"

"No, Callie," Leslie scoffed. "We're the babysitters. Your husband is taking you away."

Callie threw up her hands. "Excuse me? We don't have any plans."

I moved over and put my arm around her. "Yes, baby we do." It took a moment for her to register what I said.

"The blindfold," she began.

"Is for you," I finished. "We're going somewhere special tonight and I wanted to keep it a secret."

Tears welled up in her eyes. "You planned this?"

"For a long time," I said chuckling. "At least six weeks, maybe longer."

She looked at her mom and stepdad with disbelief. "You knew about this?"

Tony smiled. "Yes and we've been looking forward to spending some time with our grandson."

Leslie wrapped her arms around Callie and said softly, "Go be a wife for a while."

I took the blindfold from her hand and wrapped it around her eyes. "Now the adventure begins."

****

Callie

As Justin wrapped the blindfold around my eyes, not only did I feel relief that it wasn't part of some game he was playing with someone else, I was excited that it was for me. I'd been so disappointed the night before when he essentially blew me off but now I was shivering with anticipation at what he had planned. I let him lead me out of the apartment and down to our car. I wanted to ask him so many things but stopped. He'd obviously put a lot of thought into this and I was just going to let it happen. He opened the car door and gently eased me in before buckling me up. I could smell the fragrance of roses inside the car and I took a deep breath enjoying the wonderful aroma. He got in beside me and put his hand on my thigh giving it a reassuring squeeze. "You doing okay?" He asked softly.

"Yes, I'm very excited." I settled back into the seat and focused on the songs on the radio. After a few minutes, I realized he'd hooked up my iPod, the selections were all my favorite songs. I couldn't keep the smile off of my face and I felt his hand touch mine and then he clasped his hand in mine. We rode in silence with the music swirling around us and truthfully I lost track of time. I couldn't tell where we were going and I really didn't care. I was with Justin and that was all that mattered.

Eventually, Justin's driving pattern changed and I could tell we were in traffic. Within a few minutes I could tell we had pulled off the road into what I assumed was a parking lot. He stopped the car and told me, he'd be right back.   I heard some voices and then my door opened with a whoosh of air. He unbuckled my seatbelt and took my hand, helping me out of the car. I could tell we were in a parking garage because it was cool and there were echoes of other cars. He led me a few feet and we stopped. "Elevator," was all he said.

I heard a ding and we were moving again to stand inside the elevator. The doors closed and I could hear soft music playing. Justin slipped his arm around my waist and pulled me close. I felt the elevator come to a stop and the familiar ding again. The doors opened and still holding me, Justin led me across a carpeted surface. He stopped and I heard him unlocking and then opening a door. "Almost there," he whispered right next to my ear, his breath warm on my neck.

He led me into what I assumed was a hotel room from what I had heard. He walked me across the room and I felt a chair at the back of my knees. I instinctively sat and found myself sinking into a huge easy chair. "I'm almost ready," he said stepping away from me. A few minutes passed and I could hear him moving around in the room. My heart was beating wildly with anticipation but I was patient. This was going to be so worth the wait. I sensed him close to me again and felt my breath quicken as he started untying my blindfold and finally he was pulling it away from my eyes. It took a moment for my eyes to adjust but when they did, I was speechless. We were in the suite where we had our first date but it was totally transformed.   There were candles surrounding the bed which was covered in hundreds of red rose petals. In the center of the bed was a wicker basket full of fresh fruit and a champagne bucket complete with bottle of champagne and two champagne flutes. I stood on shaky legs and walked over to look at the other items surrounding the basket. A box of my favorite chocolates was arranged next to a silver tray with strawberries dipped in white chocolate. Justin came up behind me and wrapped his arms around me. "I wanted this to be perfect…just like you."

"Justin," I said breathlessly, "this is breathtaking." I leaned back against him turning my head to find his beautiful lips. We shared a slow, intimate kiss and I could feel my body responding to just being this close to him.

I turned in his arms to wrap mine around his neck but he pulled away. "Not yet, babe." He reached into a bag that was next to the bed. It was a beautifully wrapped present and I was hesitant to destroy such gorgeous wrapping paper. "I promise you what's inside is more beautiful than the outside," he chuckled. "I'll be right back."

He left the room as I sat on the edge of the bed, I ripped it open. Nestled in tissue paper was the most amazingly sexy lingerie I'd ever seen. It was a halter style baby doll nightie accented with sequins and beads. I lifted it from the box and saw it was translucent. I heard Justin come back into the room and he smiled when he saw my face. "I take it you like my taste?"

"Oh gosh, it's gorgeous," I said standing to give him another kiss. "Am I supposed to go 'slip into something more comfortable' now?" I purred.

"Actually, there's something else you need to enjoy first." He took me by the hand and walked me back to the bathroom which was enormous. The room was candlelit and in the middle of the room was an enormous garden tub full of bubbles. A white fluffy robe was laid out next to the tub along with a pair of slippers. The bath looked heavenly since I'd had to basically take showers for weeks following Ryder's birth and I was dying to sink into the bubbles.

"Are you going to join me? There's plenty of room," I said giggling.

"No, babe, this is for you. I'm going to finish preparing the rest of your evening. You take your time and enjoy." He left and I slipped out of my clothes and into the fragrant warm water. Sinking down in the bubbles, I felt my body relax instantly and I lay my head back against the side of the tub. I closed my eyes but felt myself getting drowsy, so I got up out of the bath and grabbed the robe which I wrapped myself in. I scooted into the slippers and walked over to the vanity which held my favorite lotion and perfume. I applied the lotion all over and it felt so good and smelled even better. I gave myself a spritz of perfume and then slid on my beautiful nighty.   I looked in the mirror and saw a sexy woman. Sure, I was a mom now but there was still a woman inside who was desperate to show her husband how much she loved him. I opened the door and walked out into the bedroom to find Justin in a robe waiting for me. "Are you hungry?" He asked taking my hand. I knew he'd gotten dinner because I could smell something amazing and my tummy did a tiny growl in response. "Guess so," he laughed.

I grinned and nodded. "I haven't had time to eat today," I admitted.

"Well, let's go out on the balcony and have something to eat then. We'll need some sustenance for our evening and plus your tummy growling is loud!" We walked out onto the balcony and as it was now late in the afternoon, the sky was turning beautiful shades of pink and orange. Justin pulled out my chair at the table which was beautifully set, accented with a single rose in a vase. He uncovered the dishes and I was expecting to see 'our' food but this time there were lobster tails perched next to our filet mignon accompanied by fresh vegetables and a baked potato. My mouth watered at the sight as they were my favorite but not something you get to have every day. Justin put his fork into the lobster and dipping it in the warm butter, he brought it to my mouth. A little of the butter dripped down my chin but he was there quickly kissing it away and I felt a shiver at the intimacy of the gesture. He continued to feed me little bites and finally I had to ask, "Aren't you going to eat?" I laughed.

"I have to make sure my woman is satisfied first! I read that in a magazine," he said cheekily.

Blushing, I couldn't respond. After a few more bites, I had to push his hand away. He smiled and I watched as he finished the meal. He was so adorable and I loved the way his dimples flashed when he chewed. I'd seen those dimples already on our son and knew he was going to be very popular with the ladies if he worked them just right. He wiped his mouth with his napkin and stood. "I have a gift for you." He reached under the table and pulled out a gift bag.

I removed an envelope from the bag which I ripped open to reveal a gift card with a very generous balance to use at my favorite spa. I smiled thinking of how many massages that would give me. Justin reached in the bag for the next gift. It was a jewelry box and he smiled as he opened it and I saw a beautiful pendant with Ryder's birthstone set in it. The polished peridot winked in the candlelight and that's when I noticed a key hanging on the chain with it. Puzzled, I unclasped the chain and removed the ordinary key from it and looked at Justin for an explanation. "You need to look in the bag for what the key fits."

I reached back into the gift bag and pulled out a picture frame wrapped in tissue paper. I unwrapped it to see a beautiful house with the words, 'Home Sweet Home' written on it. I couldn't breathe. "You bought a house?"

"I bought us a home," he said taking my free hand. "I bought a home that we can raise our family in and have our friends visit us. As a matter of fact, it's right up the street from Jay and Jane."

I squealed and grabbed him planting a big kiss on his mouth. "Justin, it's perfect! I can't breathe." I felt the tears welling up as I looked at the house we would grow old in.

Justin stood. "So, now that you have been pampered and showered with gifts, are you totally full or do you think you'd like to share some strawberries with me?"

I jumped up out of the chair and started toward the bed. "I'm never too full for chocolate! You know me better than that," I said grinning.

He started rubbing his hands together. "Ah, my plan to lure her closer to the bed is working," he said as he waggled his eyebrows.

I picked up a strawberry by the stem and held it out. "You first."

He walked over and holding my hand in his, took a bite of the strawberry. I snuck in a kiss and he chuckled. "I guess I got lured, huh? I'm so easy."

I laughed at his sheepish expression. "That's what I love about you, Mr. Brisson. You're easy."

He wrapped me in his arms and gave me a toe-curling kiss and as I melted in his arms, he pulled us both down among the rose petals. He rolled toward the nightstand where the champagne was chilling in the bucket and poured us each a glass. Handing me the glass, he took his and clinked it to mine. "To my beautiful wife who will always have my heart. You've made my life complete and I can only pray God grants me a long life so I can spend it with you."

I was speechless for a moment. Looking at the gorgeous man in front of me, I realized all of my dreams had come true. He loved me. Plain old ordinary Callie was gone. I was Callie Brisson, the wife of this totally hot man in front of me. I downed the glass of champagne leaned across him to put my glass down and gave him a breath-stealing kiss. He turned the tables on me by grasping the back of my neck and holding me for an even longer kiss leaving my senses reeling. We were unhurried and I could sense a change in our intimacy. We were closer than we'd ever been and I knew this was how it was supposed to be. With each touch, each caress, we showed each other just how much we loved one another. Our bodies were in perfect harmony, our hearts synchronized. We got lost in each other's eyes until we fell from the heavens holding so tightly to one another, never wanting to let go.

Epilogue

Four years later

Callie

I heard the sound of car doors slamming and I ran to see who had pulled into the driveway. It was Emily and she had her hands full of presents. I ran to grab them while yelling out, "Jane, it's Mimi!" Jane came out of the house carrying plates of food to put on the picnic table. I helped Emily get her things safely onto the gift table and then I ran to help Jane put her stuff down.

"Babe? The grill's almost ready," Jay called out as he and Justin manned the cooking area. "Can you get the hamburgers and hot dogs in a few minutes?"

Jane waved to them and under her breath said, "Are your husband's legs as useless as mine?"

Laughing, I replied, "Apparently. They must think we have nothing else to do here."

"Mama! Aunt Callie! Ryder has his head stuck in the dog door," Jolene said, running up.

"Leave it to my kid to get his head stuck in your dog door. I guess Angel should have been a bigger dog so he could use it." I went over to find Ryder with his body sticking out and his head wedged in the dog door. He was pulling and grunting and I knelt down beside him putting my hand on his back. "Baby, you need to quick struggling. Let me help you." I got him to turn his head slightly and I saw his head start to back out. Within a few minutes I had him free and he grinned flashing those dimples at me.

"I wouldn't fit, Mom," he said matter-of-factly.

"No kidding. I think you need to leave that door to Angel, okay?" He nodded and I patted him on the butt sending him off to play. I walked over to the Pak 'n Play to check on Carter. He was sleeping peacefully and his pacifier was just barely in so I eased it out then had to stifle a giggle watching his lips still moving in the sucking motion. He looked so much like Ryder when he was a baby but I knew he was going to be a handful just by the way he pitched a fit if I was just a minute late with his bottle.

"Callie, can you please help get my kids cleaned up?" Jane asked balancing two plates of hot dogs and hamburgers.

I walked over to the sandbox where Olivia was pouring sand over the head of her two-year old brother Ethan. Olivia, being two years older, tormented him by taking his toys yet he followed her around like a puppy. Ethan had been a whoopsie baby but it was a good thing because he and Olivia were growing up close. Jolene was celebrating her ninth birthday and was so mature that she was like a little mother to the two of them. She and Ryder were inseparable and since we only lived down the street, they played together a lot. "Livie, let's keep the sand in the sandbox, not on Ethan's head, okay?" I said picking Ethan up while a cascade of sand fell from his head. "Jane, I think this one's a wash job," I said looking at the sand in every crevice of his face including his ears.

Jane threw up her hands and laughed. "Jay, honey? Can Justin handle the grill for a minute while you wash your child? I have a ton of things to do before everyone else gets here."

Jay handed off the spatula with a salute, jogged over to me and scooped Ethan out of my outstretched hands. "Thanks for rescuing him, Callie. His sister loves to try to bury him in the sand."

I heard voices and realized my parents had arrived. Mom and Dad were carrying several presents and as I walked up to them I said, "You realize you don't have to buy presents for all the kids when we're celebrating one birthday."

My mom looked at me like I'd grown three heads. "Callie, how can you be so cruel. The little ones don't understand that they don't get a present so I give them one to open."

I backed away holding my hands up in surrender. "Okay, I'm not going to argue with you but you spoil them."

"As a good nana should," she huffed. She walked away to place the presents on the gift table and dad put his arm around me.

"You know you're not going to win against your mother. I've found that out," he said laughing. I nodded in agreement.

A few minutes later, Justin's parents came walking around the corner holding an equally large amount of presents. We were so blessed with parents who didn't listen. Joe and Dianne put theirs down and I saw my mom mentally counting them in her head and then a smile of satisfaction. They'd brought enough for everyone and passed the Leslie test.

Jane's former neighbors, Maegan and Nate with their triplets arrived and within moments the squealing drowned out most conversation. Jolene was showing them her gift table and I saw the girls eyeing Ryder who was acting totally uninterested.

Jane's parents came out of the house and there was another round of greetings and handshakes. Paul and Sharon had eventually moved from Portland finding North Carolina weather more agreeable to them. They'd bought a house in nearby Weaverville which was only about a twenty minute drive for them and they loved it.

Jay came out of the house with a squeaky clean Ethan and Jolene had gotten Olivia out of the sandbox and had her sitting at the kiddie table already. We all sat down and were about to eat when we saw Mrs. Callahan, oops correction, the now Mrs. Taylor and her husband Marvin coming into the backyard. I still hadn't gotten used to her new name even though they'd been married for two years now. Apparently, Mrs. Callahan had finally broken down and proposed to Marvin and he happily accepted. They'd bought my condo and moved across the hall to have more room. "Did we miss anything?" She called out.

Jane laughed, "No, we're just getting started. Dig in everybody!" The crowd was buzzing with voices as everyone grabbed food and drinks and found a place to eat. I saw Carter was still fast asleep so I grabbed a plate and gobbled down a quick burger before Mr. Demanding woke up.

After we'd all eaten until we were stuffed, it was time for Jolene to open her presents. She walked up to the table and studied the different sized boxes before settling on a little one. She turned around and held it up. "This one's from Mr. Tyler in Portland! He always remembers my birthday!" Jane's eyes met mine and I gave her a little smile. Tyler had sent Jolene a gift every year without fail on her birthday and in return, Jane sent him pictures of her as she grew older. Tyler had married Cailynn and they had a child of their own. He'd gotten himself clean and was doing really well. He'd gotten a good job despite his previous problems and was moving up in the company.

Jolene ripped open the little box and inside were a pair of earrings. "Mama, they're pierced earrings! Can I please get my ears pierced? Please?" She looked up at Jane working those big blue eyes.

Jane pondered for a moment then said what I always said, "Ask your dad."

Jay, who was chatting with Justin about some work-related project looked startled to hear his name. "Ask your dad what?"

Jolene ran over to him and threw her arms around his neck. "Please Daddy, can I get my ears pierced? Please?"

I saw him begin to say no but the batting eyes and pouting lips worked their magic on him. "I guess it's okay."

"YAY! I love you Daddy…and Mama, too." She was such a good girl and very smart too. She loved to read and I knew that Jay and Jane had gotten her an iPad for her birthday but she hadn't gotten to that present yet.

She got back to business opening her presents and she even handed out the ones to the little kids. Carter got a present too but he wasn't interested. He'd woken and immediately wanted his bottle which Justin magically produced. I sat down holding him and as he gazed up at me with his daddy's blue eyes I felt a sense of peace and happiness come over me. I looked around at my family and our friends and took the time to appreciate the love surrounding me. My best friend Jane and I had come a long way together, our lives lovingly intertwined and I knew that we'd always be there for each other through the good times and the bad. The journey through life with the ones you love is never long enough, it is meant to be shared forever.

Forever by Design

The End.

www.ingramcontent.com/pod-product-compliance
Lightning Source LLC
Chambersburg PA
CBHW070554130626
46556CB00001B/157